A DARK FANTASY HORROR ROMANCE

BLOOD MOON KISSES

ENEMIES TO LOVERS

A.L. SECORD

BLOOD MOON KISSES:

ENEMIES TO LOVERS

A DARK FANTASY HORROR ROMANCE

WRITTEN BY: A.L. SECORD

DARK FANTASY WEREWOLF MAGIC PUBLISHING

Thank you to my friends and my Sullivan and McEwen family that love and support me. A Big Thank you to: God; Trinity and Tori Secord; Andrey Trushin; Theresa McEwen, Brad Sullivan; Ellen Sullivan; David Fox; Shelley Druet; Annie and Jim Bishop, and Kent and Megs Garlough. Thank you to my fans from all of my heart and soul.

DARK FANTASY WEREWOLF MAGIC PUBLISHING Copyright © 2025
This book is available in eBook, and print formats.

Edited by: APRIL SECORD
Book Cover design by: APRIL SECORD

EBOOK ISBN: 978-1-998151-17-2
PAPERBACK ISBN: 978-1-998151-18-9
HARDCOVER ISBN: 978-1-998151-19-6

First Edition: JULY 2025
10 9 8 7 6 5 4 3 2 1

CHAPTER 1

ALORA

"Don't move old hag or you're dead!" The boy shouted.

"I am not an old hag. I am a little girl, stupid boy!" I shouted back.

"Hush now tavern wench this is serious." The boy said more severe.

The arrow swooshed through the air cutting through my golden curls straight into the serpent in the grass, I had not seen a moment before.

"You are most welcome wench, you can pay me in a kiss and I'll be on my way." The most obnoxious pale blue elf-brat of a boy was speaking but I was trying not to let on how terrified I was of snakes.

"I will not kiss you because I am not a tavern wench. I am a Princess. My name is Princess Alora of the kingdom of Camelot-Gardenia. I am royalty. I can't believe a peasant boy saved my life. I shall have to tell my Father. He's very rich and will reward you handsomely." I said a little more forthright and then really studied this fantastical elf boy that was actually kind of cute.

"Well I am not a peasant. I am Prince Dorian of the woodland elves of the Graystar Kingdom and you are trespassing on my Father's land who hates humans. Stupid girl have you any idea how dangerous these forests are? Any magical creature could curse you or worse gobble such a pretty thing like you up." As he spoke he placed his bow over his shoulder and enchanted me with his whimsical fanged smile.

He intrigued me. Here he was roaming the forest by himself and a Prince. There was no way my Father would ever let me be alone in the woods and yet here he was slaying poisonous snakes. *Too bad he's so infuriating or else I might think him a dashing handsome Prince rescuing me like that.* My thoughts were not becoming of the lady I was supposed to be as I couldn't help but stare at the tribal tattoo he had across his chest.

"Prince Dorian I think you are exaggerating the circumstance in which you found me. I'm positive I could have handled that small snake by myself. These woods are no more dangerous than my old witch of a governess who used to make me take cod liver oil." I said this with a defiant look but cringed as he grabbed the twenty foot long snake and took a bite sucking out the intestines.

"Tis' good snack, if you would like I would make an exception and share some food for such an odious beast as yourself human girl." He said and grinned with his fangs as bright as his purple eyes.

"No thank you dark elf, but I guess you did save my life just now. In these same woods, I have never seen a unicorn, a sprite, or even a water dragon. I have played in these forests since I was a very small child and you are the first magical creature I have ever seen. You are much more muscular than the story books tell and you have a rather long nose and roguish dimpled chin. Who would have thought an evil elf would be such a courageous hero." I said and rolled my eyes at him continuing to suck the meat out of the snake and leave a hollow skin.

"Yes, I know I am quite valiant and very handsome. But enough about me; let me take you safely back to your cottage. You really are far from where you would normally haunt." He said and I was taken back by his pale blue offered hand.

I could see the nails held mud and a little blood. Whose blood was another question? Although he was peculiar with his long ears and long blonde hair. I trusted his kind purple eyes. He was just too magical and wonderful to leave in the heat of the morning, even if he was the most dirty and vile boy on the face of this flat earth.

"Well I was thinking, maybe we could hang out a little longer? You are the very first dark woodland elf I have ever met. I have my dreadful etiquette studies and then harp lessons to return to. Please Prince Dorian can you take me with you and show me your part of the woods and your favorite places? I know I should get back and I will with such a valiant warrior leading the way; but after we have some fun first. What shall ye say, oh noble Prince Dorian of the grand kingdom of Graystar?" I said and giggled as I took his warm hand.

I watched the pale blue skin on his cheeks turn a pretty pink shade and then he looked away. *I knew flattery would work. Oh Prince Dorian I can have you wrapped around my finger just like the other boys of the court.* I thought and tried to hide my mischievous smile as he started to silently lead me through this little path into the woods.

"Well I guess we could go fishing or swimming in my favorite place which holds a lake monster. But if you stay with me you'll be safe. I am not needed back in my kingdom for hours. Besides none of my other friends are here. They wanted to pick on some hobgoblins and I cannot stand that kind of cruelty." He spoke sincerely and I rather enjoyed my hand in his as he continued to lead me through the woods.

He was right. I had never seen this part of the forest ever. I really was further away from my camp then I had thought I was. He paused for a moment placing his bow and quivers beside a very large oak tree. While we paused I became breathless as I watched the miracle of some unicorns grazing in the field beside the forest tree line where we stood.

Then immediately he took my hand again as we walked towards thick bracken. I graciously held his hand that seemed to glow every now and then. He started telling me stories about talking rabbits and dancing werewolves. This was the fantasy world I had read and dreamt about but never seen in real life. It was peaceful but full of life. I was in quiet awe as I watched some fairies sprinkle pixie dust over flowers that bloomed.

Even though in my Father's eyes he was the enemy, I couldn't help but see him as an equal and a best friend. But liking him meant hurting my kingdom which I could never do. So today I was pretending we were two regular humans talking and walking in the woods. *I kind of hate the fact he is really pretty for a boy and he has a sense of humor. None of the human boys were as clever or as gracious. It kind of makes me a little jealous knowing he is this free whereas I have to be escorted around everywhere. Just because I am the King's only daughter, I guess makes me some kind of wilting flower. If my Father only knew I was walking with an elf he'd lock me in the tower. But at least I could say I had today to run around with an evil wild boy that I tamed.* I thought this but then focused in on the joke Dorian was saying about unicorns having bright rainbow colored snot and laughed even though it was more gross that funny.

Dorian while holding my hand had now gotten his flute out of his small satchel and played for me. He paused every now and then to softly sing in his elvish language such a charming melody I became breathless at his magnificence. He was now skipping with me as we danced through his path through the woods. He was so strong as he held my hand in one of his hands, lifting me as I stumbled. All the while he remained singing and playing his flute in-between lovely strings of words I had no idea the meaning. It was just too magical a scene and straight out of a perfect fairytale.

When Dorian turned to me he smiled as his purple eyes glowed and started singing to me while I blushed. *Looks like I am wrong about Prince Dorian. I feel my heart's string is completely wrapped around his finger. He is such a handsome, wonderful but stupid boy. I feel he really might be my only best friend.* I thought as he smiled sweeter at me but continued to sing as I felt my heart flutter happily.

I watched as he used magic to make the flute play by itself and levitate in front of us with this green mist of magic as we skipped in the woods. Dorian was then telling me about every tree spirit he knew and the flower magic of the roses in these woods; meanwhile I hung off every word of his silvery voice that enchanted me.

🌿🌿🌿

CHAPTER 2

DORIAN

Here I was speaking and now singing sweetly to a child born of the enemy. I don't know what the matter with me was, but I felt my heart skip beats in seeing this lovely pink shade spread across her cheeks. It was like I wanted to sing all the ancient songs to her just so I could see her pretty blue eyes light up. She was so strange and fragile. I have never seen such splendor. She was in fact my age of thirteen, being born of a Daughter of Eve in the springtime, which made her older than me. So technically she was an old hag as far as I was concerned and very stupid for a girl. She knew absolutely nothing of magic or this part of the woods. But it was nice to have met such an exquisite creature. I could foresee us being the best of friends. She was so easy to be around.

Alora held no magic but I was mesmerized by her beauty.

There was only one human lullaby that I had learnt and sang it for her to see her smile more radiantly. She now joined me in singing and our voices made the woods even more magical. I knew she had caught me blush more than once and it was so uncharacteristic of me. But her eyes were the prettiest blue that made me want to share my whole world with her.

She was just more adventurous than any of the girl elves of the court. I knew she was a danger to my very soul as she started telling me about the boring fashions and attitudes of her kingdom. To speak of such things in my kingdom was a punishment of banishment or death. But here this stunning creature was so openly putting down how stupid the war was; and certain dull academic subjects she was taught; and the very wicked maids she had.

Her eyes were such a heavenly blue but every now and then I got just a hint of a tone in her voice and I knew she was just humoring me. She still thought I was stupid. But that was okay. I was used to the games that humans play because all of the magical creatures did as well. Still it was fun just to see her hold her tanned hand in mine. It was weird. I felt special and like I needed to see her smile. I needed to hear her contagious laughter that reminded me of a sweet song in the summer breeze; even after I had placed my flute back in my satchel.

I saw something else for one moment even though she was teasing me about my constellation birthmark. I saw her royal mask fade away and heard her heart beat faster as she touched the raised markings of my ancestral tattoo. She had been mocking me but from that moment on, I seen the spark in her eye for me. *I really am her hero. I heard her thoughts and I think she is right. She is my best friend.* I thought as I held her hand as we skipped.

I continued to lead her through the forest where the magic wild roses overgrew and the scent lingered on your skin for days after walking through.   The roses were supernaturally grown filling the air with harmony and love. It was not my intention to weave a spell on her but I was positive she had been weaving a spell on me.

The bushes and bushes of thorns and blooms stretched on; tearing both our royal garments. Her royal red dress was slightly torn around the hem as was my blue trousers and white plumed shirt. But the sight was worth it as we came to the edge of the hillside overlooking the enchanted lake.

"Dorian this is more stunning than any of the lakes in my kingdom." She said and I could hear her breathless awe.

"This is it. This is my home away from the dreary castle. This is where I want to live. It is far away from the court and all the wars. This is the only place I can be free. I have no one judging me and there are no rules I have to follow. I can just be myself and converse with nature just like the ancient woodland elves used to do." I said as I started taking off my boots and trouser pants.

"Dear Princess you might be too fragile for this way into the lake, so you can follow the path down the hill and I will meet you below in the water. You have to grab the rope, run and swing while letting go. It might be too hard for you, most precious Princess. Only the toughest of warrior elves enter the lake this way." I said as I discarded my long shirt on the grass leaving just my royal undergarment loin cloth on.

I beat my chest doing a wolf howl and was just about to grab the rope when Alora, now in her undergarment shirt and pantaloons, stole the rope from me. Then she ran and let go with a scream.

"Alora!" I yelled and then seen her smiling and laughing down below in the water.

"Come down Dorian the chicken. It looks like I am much braver than you great warrior elf of the chickens." She yelled up to me just as I had let go.

I cannon-balled her with the wave of my splash. No one could deflate my ego like that and get away with it. Now she was laughing and I started laughing too, completely forgetting about my revenge as I saw her smile. We splashed each other and I let her win as she got me good quite a few times. I almost drowned with laughter as she pummeled me with water. *She's so cute trying to be tough.* I thought as we swam in the lake filled with glittering light.

Swimming with her felt like magic feeding my soul. I realized my Father was wrong about the humans. I just could not see Alora growing older and killing me and my kind. And I definitely did not think she would eat me.

We teased each other and swam farther and farther in the cool waters. It was turning out to be a perfect day. I said a little enchantment and a small rainbow appeared over us wherever we swam.

"Oh Dorian, the rainbow is so lovely. I had always wanted to see one in person. It is like I could touch the colors." Alora said as she reached out beside me to touch the magic.

"You can touch the rainbow. Tell me what the color purple feels like?" I asked her and then smiled as she reached.

"I cannot tell you what the color purple feels like, but I can tell you the color red feels like my heart right now in this moment. It feels special, like an endearment perhaps." She said and I had to look away but I knew she caught my blush again.

"Dorian, why don't you discard your crown? You could place it beside mine on the hilltop shore, along with my dress and corset. It is a little silly to still have a jewel encrusted crown on your head when you are not wearing anything except your loin cloth." Alora said and giggled making me blush even more.

"Stupid human girl, don't you know anything about royal woodland elves? My crown is infused into my skin. It grows as I do. I am born with it. It cannot be removed unless forcibly. And another thing we are neither dark nor light; we are the balance of nature magic." I giggled and rolled my eyes at her curiosity.

"Oh Dorian, they don't teach humans about woodland elf lore. Do they teach elves about human lore?" She asked and then floated on her back.

"I suppose they do not, other than humans are evil. Oh look at that cloud it looks like a giant mountain spider." I said and floated beside her as she giggled.

"Simply dreadful Dorian, do they really have spiders that big? Oh look that cloud looks like a unicorn." She said and pointed as I agreed with her.

"Alora we should swim back now. We are going too close to that dark side of the lake. My Father has told me that I am never to swim there. He told me to beware of the darkness that lives there. It has claimed many elven lives." I said and pointed to an area where there were unnatural-calm dark waters.

There were strange and horrific pink lily pads. That was an abnormal flower blooming over the dark spot of happiness in the sweet melodic waters.

"Oh pish-posh Dorian, my Father said elves like tricking people. I'm sure I am strong enough to overcome the lake monster. What type of items do you have stored down there? Is it some buried treasure?" She said giggling and defiantly started swimming towards the dark water.

"No Alora, please come back. Do not go over there. I don't know if I am strong enough to fight the darkness to save you. It is forbidden for the living to linger there. That water would take you to the underworld where they will dine on your flesh. Please do not swim any further, I am coming to save you." I called out to her while reaching my hand to hers in seriousness.

Now both of us were moving towards the darkness; but one of us was giggling while the other was fearful. And I don't have to tell you which one I was as my heart raced. I could feel myself sweating under the guise of the water.

"See nothing is happening. Look at us both here surrounded by the dark water and we are fine. Pick me a flower Dorian that I can keep for all times?" She had finished saying just as I grabbed her hand.

But then something pulled her down and me with her. We were being dragged to the bottom of the lake and although I could hold my breath to the point I could be classified as part mermaid; Alora could not.

🌾🌾🌾🌾

Alora's lovely blue eyes finally fluttered open into mine, just as my mouth was against her soft lips. I had been trying to breathe for her for quite some time as she coughed and then puked all over me.

Immediately I sat her up, carefully leaning her against my chest so her head could rest on my shoulder as she coughed. I gently rubbed her back but embraced her because I was just so grateful she was part of the living world again.

"What happened Dorian? I feel awful. I remember the monster had me and then the darkness over took me. It was so cold." She said and shivered as I hugged her.

"Alora you are so stupid. You died on me. I told you not to swim there. Now look at us. My leg resembles the monsters chew toy. My Dad is going to take a strip off my hind-quarters if he finds us here. And both our kingdoms might be looking for us. It took me a long time to bring you back to life Alora." I said so stern but hugged her tighter as the thought of losing something I had just found really made my heart ache.

"What do you mean? You have completely saved my life Dorian, you are my hero." She said and then embraced me tighter as she gazed deeply into my eyes.

Her eyes were paler and softer as they filled with tears. Then she surprised me as she started kissing my blushing cheeks in thanks over and over.

"Alora the gypsies came and stole our clothes and your human crown. We are in trouble. And I have lost one of my rubies." I said while I was still worried from the assault of heavenly kisses.

"We will find the ruby together Dorian. Don't worry." She spoke softly as she sat there in my arms and we both just held each other.

"Alora you don't understand, the crown is a part of me. Do you not realize it is forbidden for us to even be here in this moment and to have played together all day?" I said as she held me and I couldn't help but plant my face in her golden curls breathing in her meadow scent of roses and lavender.

Just then she stole my breath as she looked into my eyes and kissed her soft lips to mine so deeply that I felt my soul stir in love. At first I froze and trembled. Then I surrendered to the sweetest kiss escaping my lips to hers; and a pure love I never dreamt was possible. Then I heard the noise coming from in front of us and froze.

"Alora back away from that foul dark creature right now, so I can get a clear shot of his black heart." The male's deep voice shook me to the core in its directness about killing me.

"No Daddy he saved me from drowning. He is my Prince hero." I heard the fear in her voice and felt both our heartbeats quicken as we looked into his crazy blue eyes.

"That doesn't explain where your crown is and the lack of propriety shown by you in your undergarments. Please move away from the boy so I can kill this creature of the night before he grows up and kills us one day. It is inevitable. He will become the monster that all dark woodland elves are." The human male adult looked fierce in his shiny armor and massive crown upon his head.

The tip of his arrow was directly pointed at my heart and then Alora shifted so she was completely blocking my chest with her back pressed up against me. She was sheltering me from this ogre of a man and I was surprised.

"Please Daddy...Please don't kill my best and dearest of friends." Alora was pleading as she begged for my life.

I sat there in complete shock as I felt both our heartbeats pounding like they were going to come out of the cages holding them back. But it was not the happy moment from before that kept our hearts in a race.

🌿🌿🌿🌿

CHAPTER 3

ALORA

I couldn't believe it. My Father was here at the most imprudent of times and now he was going to kill my newest dearest of friends. The only monster I have ever seen is standing here in front of me with his arrow still aimed at us. *Please don't kill the first boy that has ever kissed me Daddy. I feel my heart was floating so high just a moment before when I heard Dorian breathing sweetly in my hair as we held each other.* My thoughts slightly betrayed me as I lingered in the thought of his kiss; and felt the slight rise and fall of his chest, that I was now against in trying to shield.

"You are the first girl I have ever kissed as well Alora and now my dearest of friends. We will be okay. I know a spell that will buy us a little moment to escape. Oh and I cannot be killed by your Father that way." Dorian whispered and chanted an elvish spell.

I watched his purple eyes glow red while he was casting and then it was as if the world stopped around us.

"Dorian did you read my thoughts just now?" I asked still enamored by his stunning purple eyes.

He gently took my hand and led us away from the arrow. He smiled as he took us closer to the line of trees and the shelter of the forest.

"Of course I can read your thoughts Alora. I am a royal woodland elf. Besides that, I gave you the kiss of life and now our souls are connected until one of us perish. You might as well come home with me to my kingdom and meet my Father." Dorian said as he continued to pull me gently to the woods.

"Dorian are you mad? We are both only thirteen. Are you implying that we are engaged?" I asked now blushing as he stopped and gave me the full force of his mesmerizing purple eyes.

"Alora you won't be able to resist me. I am your soulmate now. When I brought you back to life it entangled our futures. We will both be changed because of it and neither of us will find true happiness and love with another. So it would be easier if you just come with me now. I will always take care of you. Search your heart and you will feel my love inside. And hurry the spell I just cast will wear off any moment now." Each time Dorian spoke I grew more and more bewitched by him.

I wondered as he kissed my hand while deeply looking into my eyes. *Is he right? Am I falling in love with him?*

"Of course you are Alora. Each time we hear each other's voice it will stir up the emotions your soul and heart will crave in time. You will not be able to live without me. It is the way of the elves and fairy folk." He spoke again and I had to try and force my heart to stop from being swept away into the magical woods with him.

"Dorian you must not read my thoughts ever again, even in our friendship, okay? It means a lot that I can think about things in private.

That is a human girl trait; that I need." I said and he smiled sweetly and nodded.

"I promise you I will not read your mind ever again, after today. But we really must get going. Any moment your Father will animate back to his grumpy self and we need to be long gone." He spoke again and I started shaking my head.

"I can't go. I am sorry but I am his only child. He just gets moody about me not being a proper lady yet. I cannot leave him because my mother is gravely ill." I said and he embraced me tight.

"Alora you have a right to live your life as you choose. I shall not take that from you. But you must know that fate will bring our paths in crossing again." He whispered as I held him tighter.

This stranger had just saved my life and even at the expense of his traditions was willing my freedom. I could feel my cheeks wet and hoped I would get to see him again. It was strange how all in one day someone could be so valuable to you. Suddenly Dorian picked a daisy and handed it to me. Then he gently wiped my tears away. *How is it that my heart is already missing yours? Is this the love I have always read in fairytales and always dreamt of?* I thought and seen him smile sweetly and nod in agreement.

"Dorian you must promise me you will never read my thoughts again." I said as I looked into his purple eyes that were softer than the white fluffiness of the clouds passing by in the blue sky.

"Do you not know anything stupid girl? Once a mighty and brave woodland elf makes a promise it is forever." He whispered as he hugged me again.

"Good then promise me once more you will never read my thoughts and then promise me we shall always be the dearest of friends." I said as I couldn't help myself from touching his ears; and then his crown full of golden branches and jewels while he smiled.

I couldn't help it I then kissed his cheek that was streaked golden from his tears. *Thank you my handsome hero Prince for saving me.* I thought as he gave me this mischievous look and then smiled so lovely I was breathless. Then he kissed my lips. His lips were wet and tasted like the sweet nectar of a wild honeycomb and I felt my heart speed up as I kissed him back.

"You have a deal Alora. But please stay away from this part of the woods. You my friend are to pretty to be captured and enslaved by my people." He said and slowly grabbed my hand to his.

I watched as his hand glowed while holding my hand. Then with a smile and a crimson blush across his cheeks; he left before I could say another word. I watched his strong muscular frame disappear into the thick forest just as I heard my Father stirring.

"Enslaved?" I whispered in puzzlement and then rested my fingers on my soft lips where his kiss lingered.

Dorian was a Prince and the first boy that had ever kissed me and he wasn't even human. *I hope the magic of his elvish kiss shall stay in my heart forever.* I thought as I looked down and found the daisy he had gave me. There on the grass beside the daisy was this large glowing crimson ruby. I quickly hid both items in my little pocket of my pantaloons before my Father turned to me.

"Where has that evil elven boy gone?" His stern voice made me tremble.

"I'm not sure Daddy, must have been royal elven magic." I said as my Father wrapped his royal red cloak around me.

"What an ungentlemanly thing to do. Of course, what can you expect from such wild savages as dark woodland elves? Let us leave this place quickly. Your mother will be worried sick if I do not bring you home at a decent hour. Not to mention the court cannot eat until our arrival." My Father said as he placed me on his horse and then he mounted.

"Alora you look quite pale, are you feeling alright? I know that you both must have been into some kind of trouble. That boy had a nasty bite on his leg." He said so deep in perspection it made me wonder if he was concerned because he was of course a Father first and then a King.

"I am quite well Father. Prince Dorian had saved me from this lake monster. Let us be gone from this dreadful place. I do feel rather sleepy all of a sudden and there seems to be a touch of autumn air through the forest." I said as my eyes started to flutter in closing and then I heard my Father bellowing.

"Alora! Alora!" I could feel his strong arms holding me tightly as we galloped.

Then the memory of swimming and laughing with a crowned elvish boy; shrouded me into the darkness of a cold emptiness.

🌾🌾🌾

CHAPTER 4

DORIAN

The castle seemed to have an air of foreboding as I shivered while keeping my head low. The cold cobblestones seemed like a false sense of sanctuary from the heat of the summer. But I was perspiring from being in my Father's presence and knowing he had read my mind before I had even had a chance to cross the moat of the kingdom.

Now here I was barely even dressed in my finest and already on my knees in the lowest of bows in pleading for compassion from a heart that lacked anything but enforcing laws. There were no guards here and yet I was being placed on trial because we were at war with the elf-eating humans.

I closed my eyes and thought about Alora's shimmering curls in the sunshine that flecked a golden hue like the finest of treasures. Not any of the elf Princesses had hair that sparkled into glittering light of happiness like hers did.

"Dorian Wolf Graystar VI, you have disobeyed me for the last time. I do not care that the mortal girl was drowning. We are in a war and all humans are our enemies. This is the seventeenth century; you cannot be so frivolous and carefree. You were betrothed since infantry and now look at what you have done. You are missing a ruby from your crown. And it isn't just any ruby. It is one of three from your heart center. You have placed the whole kingdom at risk all because your heart has fallen over some human girl." He bellowed as I quickly glanced and seen his eyes glowing red from the fires of Hades.

"My King, it was an accident. How was I to know it would be true loves kiss and unlock one of the rubies from my heart?" I said and bowed even lower, even though I was addressing my parents in their private tea room.

"I can't believe you would gift such a treacherous creature our most revered of gifts. The magic of the kiss of life was never to be taken for granted. It's our most sacred of matrimonial gifts and now she has your heart centered ruby. Of which by the way has to be willingly gifted back or the vile creature die. You will not even be whole without it and I cannot marry you off when your heart belongs to another. Dorian, have you any idea the situation you have placed our kingdom in? Even looking at you disgusts me in the knowledge of your fraternization with the enemy. It's like you don't even remember the history of bloodshed between the elves and humans." He hollered as I kept my head low.

"Just look at yourself. You have changed. There is more than something different about you now. That bandage of blood on your leg. Yes, I can see though the layers of linen now. You were bitten." He said and then gasped with my Mother.

"The guards said they saw you enter the castle gate only dressed in your regal loin cloth and I didn't believe them. We are royalty Dorian. I executed them immediately when they said they smelt the darkness off your blood. Now look at what you have become. You are cursed." His deep voice now became much quieter and much more terrifying.

I trembled at what he was going to do to me. The knowledge of several executed members of the court flashed through my mind. All of them had been willingly found guilty for being in love with humans; and were brutally slaughtered.

My Queen Mother looked at me lovingly but sadly shook her head and then looked away from me. Silent golden tears were streaming down her cheek and I knew her thoughts reaching out to me had been silenced by my Father's magic. I glanced at her long silent face as she nodded in agreement to some silent decree they had come up with in punishment of their only child now a blemish on the kingdom of Graystar's magic. I watched on in horror as they both had a telepathic conversation regarding me and knew I was silenced from them.

"My mind is made up Dorian. The more I look upon you the more I realize you don't even resemble the bright, purple-eyed Son of my heart and my future successor. It is done." He calmly said and I could feel my heart beating faster.

"Father you can't be serious? It was an accident. You must search your heart and know I didn't mean to betray you. I didn't mean to fall in love with Alora." I said in despair as I looked upon my parent's cold but regal blank stares.

"Enough, you are to address me as your King. I could have saved you with my magic, but I want you to feel the weight of your actions. I want you to feel that pain each full moon's curse. Too many savage humans have slayed and eaten our kind. Now my only child has been reduced to nothing more than a common criminal, a street concubine at best. From this day forth you are banished from the castle and the kingdom. You will have no mercy from any of the woodland elves if you are found in the field. We shall slaughter you with the purest of silver arrows until you are dead then we shall sever your head, and burn your body so that you never rise up. I order you to be gone from here and never return again. And pray Dorian I shall never find you in the woods because my silver dagger will be the last thing you will ever see of this world." As my Father spoke his voice echoed throughout the castle and I looked up in terror just as he snapped his fingers.

A blaze of purple red smoke swirled around me and suddenly I was now in the woods far, far away from the magic lands of my kingdom. I was left with the dark gray cloak on my back and striped back down to the undergarments of my regal loin cloth that I had recently dressed over. I looked over to see my bow and arrows exactly where I had left them by the tree in the borderlands of the human and magic world.

"N-o-o-o-o-o-o." I yelled with uncontrollable tears cascading down my face.

But I was truly alone. No one had heard me except the other uncaring creatures who were outcast into the vast gloomy forest. I fell to my knees as I started to panic. My Father had not removed my crown but it would not buy me any friends, not in this area of outlaws. I sat with my hands covering my face knowing I had just lost everything.

Then I heard the long wolf howl and gasped as the large black-furred creature emerged like some lurking terror from behind a tree.

🌿🌿🌿

CHAPTER 5

ALORA

"Princess Alora Summer Lilith, thank you for sharing this chocolate it is divine. And this gift of silk is very gracious of your highness but what will your suitors think if they see your chamber maid in the highest of fashions that are meant for your likeness?"

"Dearest Elizabeth, I have told you time and time again; when we are alone you may just call me Alora. You are my dearest of friends besides I tire of the grand gifts from all of my suitors. Not one has tried to sweet talk my heart and turn my affection towards them." I said and sighed as my servant continued to braid my long blonde curls.

"I am so bored with being persuaded and bribed out of my family for greater fortune and jewels. I need a change before I am wed off to the highest bidder in a race for my untamable heart. I want the true magic of love that I have read in fairytales. You know sometimes I dream of this pale blue wild man in a loin cloth who brings me wildflowers while completely wooing my heart with poetry and an enchanting melody he plays on his flute." I said and sighed at the crown now being placed on my head and the braids being tucked around the gold.

"Princess Alora you mustn't speak of dreams such as these. If someone were to hear such things you would be incarcerated for such high treason. The dark elves of the woods eat humans it's a common fact and they are the only creatures I know of that have blue skin." The servant girl began to bath me and then place a new chemise and corset on me.

I sighed as I looked at all of my loveliness in the mirror, the whole time I had been being dressed. I knew I was alluring and could have any man I wanted. But I wanted adventure, mystery, and romance. I wanted to be kissed by a stranger and even have a passionate love affair before marrying my future husband. I dreamt of being wicked. I also wanted to be rescued by the man I would marry, so I would always see him handsome and brave. But none of my many suitors fit that description.

I sighed as the maid started to make my corset tighter to make my already flattering figure burst with more exuberance, the kind I really didn't need any more of. But this was the only way to catch a good husband. *I am half-dressed and yet I do not even care to pick out a lovely overdress of high summer fashion. I am so bored. I need adventure. I feel like I am missing something in my life. But what is it that is beyond my vision of my own imminent golden future?* I sighed again as I looked at myself in the mirror.

"Your highness, may I speak to you so boldly?" The maid said as she stood beside me in the mirror.

"Yes of course, Elizabeth we are in private counsel and I do treasure your friendship more than anything in the world." I said as I smiled at her and held her hand.

"Thank you your highness, I need to speak from my heart center. I have cared for you and been your consort and servant for over ten years my lady. I had come to the castle from a poor family when I was already deemed an old maid of twenty three with no prospects. Well your highness, it saddens me to see such a youthful beauty full of grace; to be suffering in silence. My wish and prayer is that you will find true happiness and that true love you are seeking. You are approaching nineteen my lady, please keep your heart open in the meantime. You never know, one of these suitors has to meet your fancy eventually. Do not wait too long though; or your Father will pick out a husband for you." Elizabeth said and she patted my hand which I was grateful for her comfort but still in a mood.

"I think that is my happiness solution that I have yet to find. Out of all of my handsome suitors none have turned my head by the magic in their gaze. I could not look at them knowing only financial gains of our conjoined kingdoms are their priority. Where is the magic of love and forbidden adventure in romance to be had in a world of cold gray walls and an even colder golden throne?" I said and frowned as I looked at the lake far in the distance.

"My lady, please do not speak like that and do not give up on your suitors just yet. There will be time to know and judge a good man's character after ye wed. The summer day is pretty maybe we could take a turn around the garden? That might persuade your character into lifting your spirits or maybe we could go to the market? I heard from the baker that the ogres were selling eels again and the sight is interesting but quite dreadful. I shall find your best day-outing dress in your old chest." Elizabeth said cheerfully and then went over to the ancient chest of dazzling silk and cotton garments especially for the likes of royal summer fashion.

She ruffled around and then gasped but I continued to stare at myself in the mirror.

"Oh my lady, I found your ruby necklace. Would you like to wear it today?" She held up the ruby and instantly it warmed my heart.

"Yes Elizabeth, this is most fortunate. This is my lucky necklace. I thought I had lost it. It is such a treasure to me and fills my heart with the much needed magic I deserve today. I think I shall wear the crimson silk dress. It is much too pretty to sit in that chest for any much longer." I said as Elizabeth helped me clasp the necklace around my lovely throat.

Then she helped me pull on the stunning red garment fit for a Princess. I twirled and admired myself in the mirror. *I look ravishing today. I hope my Father doesn't see me or else I will never be allowed to leave the courtyard.* I thought as I twirled in the mirror and Elizabeth gently fixed a loosened curl for me.

"My lady do you mind if I ask what makes the necklace lucky?" Elizabeth said and I knew she was sweet but she never read fairy tales and she never understood magical possibilities.

"Well when I was younger I became gravely ill after almost drowning by the summer cottage. My Father seemed to think this gemstone was magic and it healed me unexplainably the moment it was placed as a gift around my neck. The only thing was the fever made me forget anything from before I woke up in my castle bedroom. I asked my Father if he had given me the necklace and he said he had found the ruby in my dress pocket. So he bound the ruby in leather and made a necklace the likes for a true Princess. But he never wanted to discuss the magical properties regarding the necklace or my drowning. Ever since this necklace has brought me luck. I even feel more beautiful and lavishing wearing it." I said as I twirled again.

"My lady you look so radiant. We shall have fun counting all the men's heads and hearts you turn today." Elizabeth said as she continued to tie the ribbons on the bodice of the dress tighter and then stepped back so I could admire myself even more.

"Yes I am quite lovely but am too absurdly rich to care anymore if men stare at me. Let us leave the castle at once. I am too much in a dark state regarding my suitors and need some small freedom. Go to the cellar and fetch a bottle of ale from the vault and we shall finally have fun. Arrange the carriage quickly and we shall go to the market and purchase some more chocolate. Tell my Father we are leaving and grab us some sweets from the bakery for lunch." I said as I admired myself more.

"Yes my lady." Elizabeth said and then scurried off right before passing me the royal red travelling cloak.

🌾🌾🌾

CHAPTER 6

DORIAN

"I am so tired of rabbit. I want something I can really sink my fangs into." I said as I slammed my fist down on my small wooden table.

"Well then go to the woods and hunt the two mountain lions that have been eating my people. You know the reward handsomely pays and it would be doing your old friend some good service." The great goblin spoke and smiled as he smoked his pipe.

"Well King Lucien, it would help me to buy some much needed flour and spices from the market. I could also use the gold coins to buy some potatoes and more feathers for my arrows." I said as I reached my hand out to the already extended hand of the ancient goblin King.

As we shook hands my hand glowed as the deal was sealed. Then we both flogged back our mugs now emptied from the good mead. Then as if on cue the magical pitcher poured into our empty mugs as I drank back immediately.

"Yes, dear woodland Son you could buy even more with the gold I will give you and you would be helping me out immensely. I will pay twice. The first payment of gold is for the magical promise of the first lion slain. Then you will get the rest of the golden coins after you kill the second mountain lion. I knew you would agree. So here are the six hundred gold coins for the first mountain lion." King Lucien laughed jolly as he slammed the gold coins on the table and some spilt out in a glittering mess of happiness.

My eyes went wide in seeing that much gold in one place. It had been a long time and I had been hungered to the point of starvation in the season of autumn before the harsh winter. I was without words at the old King's generosity all these years of showing up with little jobs so that I could even live.

"I have always wanted to ask you something ever since we have been friends Dorian and now is as good as any a time for conversation. With all the magic you hold Prince Dorian, why not grow the potatoes using the magic in your blood?" King Lucien asked as he smoked his pipe while I drank another mug filled with the delicious summertime mead I had made.

"My kingdom, my King and my Queen have both shunned me and abandoned me. To use my magic to grow my food is like crawling back and begging for them to give me my life back. The magic was always my birthright but using it makes me feel like my Father has won. And I want him to know he has not. I have endured and blossomed in his absence these last six years. He could not break my will. I have learnt how to survive without magic which has saved my life from his soldiers. Even in the face of my death it would have to be pretty important to use any sort of magic." I said and drank another mug of mead in cheers with the King.

Lucien was drinking just as much and it felt good that he trusted me enough to be himself. I rather enjoyed his company and Father-like friendship. He had found me with the wolf pup, playing my flute in the meadow one day; and we had been friends since.

"Well dear woodland Son I must be off or the Queen shall slit my throat and marry the court jester. Maybe when you are in the market you could purchase some garments lad. That loin cloth of yours is looking more free for the heat of the summer but now it is also looking too ragged for your blue blood. And another thing good boy, you are starting to smell like rotting forest elderberries. Wash before you go and maybe a fine maiden will catch your wild heart. That reminds me, the ogres in the market are selling fresh eel which is quite tasty I hear." The old goblin King said and laughed.

"My odor is pleasant and I am not in need of some old hag to order me about when my heart can truly be free." I said with a dignified air and then scrunched up my nose in disgust as I caught a whiff of myself from the breeze of the window.

I watched the clever King of the goblins catch this with his keen black eyes and laugh. He raised his mug to mine and we drank as I laughed from his jolly-belly-laughter.

"First, I will kill the mountain lion and then bathe." I shouted in a toast.

"No, how about first we drink." Lucien said and I smiled.

"Yes, I will drink to that." I said as we both drank and then laughed again.

My home forged out of a giant redwood was large enough and the cupboards were bare but my table held candles and enough mead to drown out anyone's sorrows for years. I was eternally grateful for my little space which I had made my own even if it was a little in disrepair.

Then King Lucien finished his mug of mead; and waved goodbye as he sprinkled some pixie dust and vanished. I was left hearing his laughter until the dust settled. Then I smelt my skin and realized the old man was right. I grabbed my soap and went to the lake.

❧❧❧❧

CHAPTER 7

ALORA

"Tell the guards to wait by the carriage. I wish to explore the market only with you Elizabeth as my escort." I said as I discarded my crown in my bag and placed the hood of my dark crimson cloak over my head.

"Yes my lady as you wish but I do not think Talon, the captain of the guards, will allow us ladies to be alone in the market without a male escort."

"Elizabeth you worry enough for the both of us but I always have my small dagger hidden in my corset. I have never had to use it in all this time even though I am trained in the art of sword fighting and archery. I am grateful my Father wanted a Son but got me instead. Besides that the Peace Treaty will protect us." I said and smiled at Elizabeth's still worried face.

"Yes I agree my lady but I am still getting this uneasy feeling about us travelling to the other side of the market where the magical creatures can buy their goods and sell their wares." Elizabeth said and I was getting inpatient as she was the one who had even suggested us to go see the weird eel creatures to begin with.

"Enough of this talk Elizabeth. I do not wish for your opinion of fears at this time. I order you to tell the guards to stay here with the carriage this instant. And further more I wish to be addressed as Guinevere while we are out in public. I wish to travel as your companion and leave the royalty of my birth right for the day. Let us make friends with the commoners. Let us have some pleasurable informality before returning back to the gloomy castle and another feast of celebration tonight. Let us finish this good bottle of mead at once so we will have unregulated fun." I said and looked at her blue servant cloak just before she left and had a quick thought.

"One more thing, switch with me this instant your blue servant cloak with my royal red cloak. I want to be treated as a normal part of society even if it is only for today. I want an adventure. I also want to kiss a stranger in the market if only a taste of what freedom would be. And I wish for us to be absolutely loaded with mead before I have to endure getting engaged." I said and switched cloaks with Elizabeth as she looked even more worried.

"Yes my lady." Elizabeth said and then left to speak with the guards as I drank from the bottle.

I heard her ordering the guards and shutting down any objections instantly. Then she came in with a bright smile and we giggled in-between drinking from the bottle. *Today is the perfect day to find a handsome stranger to kiss.* I thought as Elizabeth helped me out of the carriage and we tried to act sober until we were far from the sights of my Father's guards. Then we giggled our way past the normal market as people bowed their heads whenever Elizabeth walked past. I felt the freedom of my caged soul calling me and it felt good to be rid of the shackles of royalty even if only for today.

"Let us go over there Elizabeth. Let us cross over to the magical side of the market and see if we can find a good tavern. Even if we cannot find tall dreamy strangers to have fun with, at least we can get good and filthy drunk before we go back to the castle." I said as Elizabeth started giggling.

❦❦❦❦

CHAPTER 8

DORIAN

I had been seated at the bar enjoying a nice posset when I saw the two humans walk into the tavern. The one in the blue servants cloak sat so close to me they knocked my arm and made me spill the lovely fluid on my gray cloak. The crowd hushed suddenly as I stood up. It was fair to say that I had a reputation of being dangerous. No one had messed with me because they all new me and my Father. Then I noticed it was a beautiful lady that had bumped me by accident, as I took off my gray cloak. I was surprised to see the humans were both unaccompanied ladies.

She quickly apologized and as soon as I heard her sweet voice something stirred in me. My purple eyes grew softer as she bought me two more drinks and gave me some gold to purchase another cloak; even though I declined. It was strange to see both ladies eyes completely all over my muscular frame. It was as if they had never seen a male woodland elf Prince before.

The way her pretty eyes were scandalously looking all over my muscular pale-blue body made me blush. She was looking at my ancestral tattoo across my chest. She was now gazing into my eyes and I felt her trying to capture my soul as I slightly turned from her. I felt her eyes on my back full of deep scars from the lashes the King of Camelot-Gardenia had given me.

My cunning eyes could see her from my peripheral vison as her pretty blue eyes had travelled to my large golden crown and then travelled back down my whole pale-blue body again; stopping on my loin cloth. Suddenly, I wished I had purchased trousers and another loin cloth as this one really was too revealing apparently. Even turning my head in her direction did not stop her stare. In this moment, I felt like I really was what my Father had said I was. This attractive human had just purchased me for two more possets as her blue eyes frolicked all over me.

I reattached my wet cloak and drank my drinks quickly. I thanked her and then left. I did not want to be around those very attractive female humans any longer than I had to be. They are a mysterious trouble that I did not want and I had already drunk too much that day for responsible choices.

🌿🌿🌿

Some time had passed but I couldn't shake the feeling I had of being gazed upon by such a beautiful blue eyed lady. As I stopped at the little chocolate stand I purchased some delicacies. Then the same annoying but beautiful servant lady in the blue cloak bumped into me again. This time she had made me drop my small satchel of gold coins. But she had picked them up for me. Her apology was too sweet as was her sensualness. My heart skipped as she offered to buy me some chocolate and I declined; but she did so anyways. I gasped as her soft hand passed me the chocolates and my small satchel of gold. I felt this electrical charge from her fingers. Then another merchant rudely pushed us together into the alley and far from the public view.

We stood there with my back against the stone wall as she held me in accident or not. Her hands were on my waist inside my cloak and she did not remove them as I became breathless. No one had held me like her hands were now, in a very long time. We were just lost in each other's eyes, gazing deeply and I felt my heart beating faster. I smelt the mead clear as day off her breath. She had this strange leather necklace on and it was completely backwards which made her a perfect beautiful mess.

I looked into her happy, mesmerizing blue eyes. Then she very carefully moved my cloak hood down to my shoulders and I did the same to her cloak hood. We didn't speak as we just gazed into each other's eyes. Her hand came to the side of my face in a caress but I shuddered at her gentle touch and her expression changed to an indescribable sadness. I felt through her gaze that she knew the world had been cruel to me and my fierceness was a big façade. Her eyes weren't just looking into my soul; they were finding a safe place in my heart.

Her golden braids were out of her cloak as she then pushed me to the wall with a fierce hunger that I had never seen from a female. She then pulled my face down to passionately kiss me. I couldn't resist her allure with as much mead and posset I had drunk that day. This was the most daring thing a magnificent human lady had ever done to me. No one this magmatic had ever dared to kiss me once they saw my golden crown on my head, but she did. And she was the most gorgeous creature I had ever beheld. I could care less about her rank in society or our unusual behavior.

To be kissed by an exquisite, blue eyed stranger was exhilarating and a sweet enthralling adventure that my soul had secretly yearned for. I tasted her soft lips and her hands went to my muscular torso sliding her way to the scars on my back. She parted my lips with her tongue and at first I was outraged; and then kissed her back tenderly. My tongue longed for hers as she tasted of the wonderful mead and chocolates.

Her sweet stolen kisses made me ache deep in my soul of something I was lacking in my life. Her hungry adoring kisses were making me lose my senses as her loving hands went everywhere and I gasped but indulged this comfort I longed for. My hands were just as scandalous as my mouth, as I nibbled and sucked on her ear lobe. I heard her moan with me as my hands flipped up the layers of her sensual red dress. She had discovered my enormous craving for her. Now we both were frantically and forbiddenly giving each other pleasure. Her kisses had found my immense sacredness and now I was trying to catch my breath. I gasped in needing what she was giving me and hadn't realized how alone I was from the wanted touch of a loving female.

I was continually breathless as I became panted and sweaty before I started to cry out. Then she sucked all of the massive volcanic eruption of pleasure out of me as my golden tears rolled down my cheeks.

I breathed heavy as I started kissing her with just as much sensualness down her cleavage and popping her glorious large bosom out of her red silk dress. *God is she ever magnificent.* I thought as I squeezed and kissed her down her body. She was heavenly as she tasted like chocolate, mead and ginger. Her mesmerizing voice was so bewitching as I heard her moaning that she wanted more of me. I wanted and watched her pleasure seeking blue eyes. Her seductive smile made me lose all good royal sense; as I detached my loin cloth and gently carried her to lay with her on some nearby hay bales in the very back of the alley. We were like two whimsical physical waves of the ocean, rocking back and forth together in perfect harmony. We matched each other's longing in squeezing and steamy kisses.

This was the likes of which I had never known as she cried out and I cried out. Not being able to subdue our primal needs we flowed together again and both erupted in a rhapsody of massive pleasure in our volcanic cries over and over. *God I need to marry this female. I don't even know her name.* Then we lay there catching our breath with her body draped over mine and holding each other lovingly; as I covered us with my larger cloak. It was as if no time was passing as she stayed in my arms holding me and still kissing me.

Suddenly she sat up worried as she needed to fix her layers and her overdress. But I helped her with her corset lovingly as she told me it had to be tighter and showed me how to tie the bows on her bodice. After she looked respectable; I tried to secure my loin cloth of which she kept teasingly untying and tempting me with affectionate touches.

We both lay back down in each other's arms completely dressed and still sweetly kissing each other. Although with her kisses, her hands continued to caress all of my body and I was euphoric as I kissed her back. I felt like her heart had found my loneliness. I felt like she was a gift from the great Goddess Fortuna in answering my prayers for a soulmate.

"You were exactly what I needed today. I am so glad to have discovered you in the tavern by Fate. But I shall have to be leaving my handsome stranger lover. My friend will be looking for me." She sweetly said as I helped her to her feet and she kissed me long and true.

My heart beat faster as I tried to speak while she kept sliding her hands back over my longing body and inside my cloak. I adored her passionate kisses and loving hands still frolicking over my wanting body even in her sweet goodbye.

"Please tell me your name. How will I find you?" I said breathless as she then kissed me tenderly while holding my hands.

"My name is Guinevere. Let us just have this sweet summer dream of mysterious romance. If Fate should bequeath us so fortunate to bring us together again in the future; then we will know we were always meant to be together." She sweetly said as she kissed and embraced me once more.

Then she left out of the privacy of the alleyway and back into the flooded crowd at the market. As soon as she was gone I had been in longing for her. *Where did my mystery female with pretty blue eyes go?*

I was still breathless as my heart started to hurt in longing for her. But her blue servants cloak matched many others; all of which wasn't hers. Making sure my cloak covered my crown I made my way slowly out of the alley. Now I sadly walked to the general store where I needed to purchase supplies and leave this place of longing. *Something so magical and wonderful has just happened to me; and all I can feel now is the sadness in my heart because of her absence.* I thought as I went into the shop.

Quickly I ordered the flour, spices, potatoes, eel meat, tea, and some magical coffee. As the ogre shop keeper gathered my stuff he started talking about the experience he had just had a moment before when he was opening the store.

"Prince Dorian I saw this human-concubine in the red velvet cloak. I heard she is the greatest concubine of all of this side of the kingdom of Camelot-Gardenia. I think I could eat that sun kissed skin of hers raw. My saliva couldn't stop dripping as she asked me if I had seen her friend in a red silk dress. She smelt of chocolate and mead. I swear it was the first time I had ever seen such a lovely female intoxicated. She was even kind to me. I had dropped an apple in my stupor of her grace and she had picked it up for me." The ogre shop keeper was talking candid to me as his ogre wife packed a few things adding them to my sack of supplies.

I just wanted to get my supplies and be out of the village. My heart had seen more excitement than I had experienced in a very long time. And it really did feel like a dream. I even questioned if she had kissed me out of loneliness or love. Either way I wanted to be gone from this place. Peace Treaty or not, I did not trust being here. The war wasn't with all magical creatures. It was only with my kind.

"Shop keeper that is fine. But I am not interested in the human and you should not be either. Female humans are dangerous." I said as I rolled my eyes.

"But Prince Dorian you should have seen her bountiful bosom. They were so full and looked much sweeter than my wife's." The shop keeper ogre said as he extended his short arms and hands in front of his chest like a giant's bosom.

"Excuse me? How dare you Treefer. We have been married for six hundred and three seasons and now you have the nerve to talk about a female human. What about your nine outstanding Sons I have produced for you?" The shop keeper's wife scolded and then stormed to the back of the store as I tried to look elsewhere while I could hear clay pots breaking.

"My darling I was only mentioning her bosom because I was hungry for juicy human meat." The shop keeping ogre rebutted but it was too late.

A full on argument was happening behind the counter now as they moved throughout the store breaking stuff. For the most part they had gone back to the very back of the store completely yelling at each other in ogre tongue and then back in English. As I stood there waiting to pay, I listened to them squawk back and forth about who was prettier. Then they started violently arguing about breaking the Peace Treaty and who they were eating for dinner tonight.

"Listen shop keeper I am leaving my three gold coins on the

counter. It should more than pay for the few supplies in my satchel. And my advice for you is to stay away from that woman charlatan. Peace Treaty or not, humans are dangerous." I said and then turned around to see the same two attractive ladies walk in just as the words left my lips.

The one female I immediately recognized. She had those mesmerizing blue eyes that left me speechless. Her dull blue cloak stood out from how desirable she really was. The other woman's red cloak was the royal colors and a dead giveaway that I should be leaving now. I needed to be out of here. I hated humans and all the royal family of the kingdom of Camelot-Gardenia. But she was too sweet and kind to be running around with such a villainous royal. I re-adjusted my gray cloak to conceal my obvious golden crown before I gathered her special attention again.

But my heart still longed for hers. I was startled when I turned back to see her sparkling blue eyes that had found mine again and her beautiful gaze left me breathless once more. Her soft hand was reaching to mine as she affectionately smiled to me and I lovingly smiled back to her. My hand was reaching for hers as well as my heart.

Just then the door swung open and an armored knight pushed me and the ladies to the ground beside each other.

"Princess Alora, please forgive me in my haste. Your father has ordered me to find you and bring you back to the castle urgently. He has agreed upon Prince Lancelot in having your hand in marriage. You will be engaged today. There will be a great feast and wedding tonight." The knight said as he helped the red cloaked woman to her feet and pulled her hard out the door.

"Wait my servant girl Guinevere is needed with me." She called out as the knight insisted her leaving.

"There is no time to waste. I have orders from the King to bring you back to the castle immediately on my gallant steed. I will bring back a carriage for your servant girl tonight after the celebrations. You are to be brought straight to your bed chambers where the other servants will get you ready for your wedding. This is a glorious day." The knight said and then pulled the royal red cloaked lady up onto his lap after he mounted.

Then they galloped away faster than the wind. Meanwhile I was left stunned at how fast this situation had changed and how they had left the poor servant girl alone on the floor. I walked over to see if she was okay and noticed the big bump on her forehead.

This poor servant girl was my mystery lady and she was unconscious. She had been completely left in a magic store owned by ogres that were arguing about eating human for dinner tonight and breaking the Peace Treaty. *Such a shame, she is such a lovely creature. I could claim her as my bride and give her a life full of love, but it might be too hard on her. It is most unfortunate she is just in the wrong place at the wrong time. I only have a few moments if I am to save her life from these ogres.* I thought just as I saw the familiar red glint from the jewel attached to the leather necklace she wore. It was the same jewel that had caused me such pain and anguish six years ago. *Finally fate has gifted me a chance to get revenge on the one who took my status, my kingdom, and my family.* I thought as I smiled more wicked than I intended and I saw myself in the mirror.

I left four gold coins on the counter and stashed some ladies nightgowns and dresses in my sack with my supplies. It was still an overpayment. Meanwhile the ogres were really fighting in the back of the store and completely ignorant of everything that had happened up front.

Ever so gently, I picked Alora up and carried her over one shoulder as I held my sack of supplies in the other. I left the building while the ogres were still too preoccupied. I was going to enjoy taking everything away from her. But I delicately carried her with my supplies as I started to head out of the market and village.

Then I saw the poor old homeless centaur and I stopped by his spot on the street. His cup was empty and his eyes were now a dull black, like all the hope had been sucked out of his life. His clothes were the same ragged materials like that of my loin cloth. I grabbed my small satchel of gold coins and without thought I gently placed the whole bag in his hand. Then I gently placed Alora down and my supplies as I took off my worn gray cloak to cover the ancient centaur up. He mouthed the words thank you and I gasped as I seen that his tongue was cut off. *This poor fellow was a victim of the war.* I thought as I gave him a nod. Then I carefully picked back up Alora and my supplies and started walking again out of the kingdom limits. I whistled loudly as my giant pet wolf ran to me and licked my fingers.

"Easy boy, we have a guest. She is going to love you like she never knew possible." I said and laughed as we started to go deeper and deeper into the forest.

The plan was too clever. The King wouldn't even know she was gone until it was too late. She would be hidden deep inside the magical boundaries and past the human limits of the castle. The only thing that I needed to do was stop my heart from growing too attached to her. She already enchanted my soul in the market when she was a stranger. *It will be really hard not to fall in love with her.* I thought as I felt her hand touch my back in her slumber and gently caress my scars. *Can my hate be stronger than the love I feel for her? I have been waiting for a chance at revenge these past six years and now the encounter with her in the alley has changed my heart. I have to be resilient and remember what joy it will bring me once I see her suffer like I have.*

🌿🌿🌿🌿

CHAPTER 9

ALORA

"Good I am so glad you are up Guinevere. You have been out for days." The deep sultry voice said as my hand went to the pain from my temple.

"What happened? You called me Guinevere. But I don't recognize that name. Actually, I do not recollect anything at this time." I said as my hand went to the tender bump on my forehead.

"You do not recall the accident? You were bathing me like usual, after you did your chores. Then you slipped and bumped your head off the floor. It is a good thing for you that I could partially heal you with my magic." His voice was deep and dreamy as he stood in the shadows across the room.

"Not to sound rude but who are you again? I am sorry but I am having a hard time in remembering anything about you or this place." I said as I looked down to the thin lace night gown I was wearing and the many torn and ragged blankets over me on the bed.

I sat up too quickly and was immediately in agony. I squinted as I seen the sun shining down through multiple windows and it revealed a large red door across the very outsized room. There was a lengthy kitchen and fireplace along one side of the room, lined with numerous windows of different shapes. Directly across the large space of wooden flooring was a small wooden table and four chairs along with more numerous sized windows that stretched to the ceiling. Each strange sized window was framed in different colors which reminded me instantly of all the different seasons of tinted tree leaves.

Then I saw him and became instantly speechless.

When he suddenly stepped out of the shadows and into the full light of the sun; I felt my heart beat faster. I never knew such handsome men existed. His amazing purple eyes looked magnetic as he raised an eyebrow at me. There was no denying his pale blue skin and long elvish ears. The only thing that was strange was this golden crown of what looked like branches sitting proud on his temple.

The glittering crown upon his long blonde hair was adorned with rubies, diamonds, and emeralds. I also noticed a little hole of an empty space amongst the gold which looked to be missing a gemstone. His regalness was undeniable with his strong dimpled chin.

I watched him walking to take the kettle off the small fire. As he moved the tattered loin cloth he wore, dangled dangerously lose. His body was lean and muscular. But I flinched at the several long scars down his back. *He has survived being tortured severely. I can see by the long lashes down his back. But how could he have survived the beating?* I thought as I watched him placing herbs in two pottery mugs and pour the hot water inside. He had made two teas and then I heard him chant a little spell making both teas and his eyes glow; as he turned to me.

He gracefully brought the mugs over and sat on the bed close to where I was seated. I had propped pillows behind myself and was leaning against the head board of the bed, along the wall. Directly past his gorgeous vision was the tub across from the bed. *He said I usually bath him?* I blushed as his smile seemed to light up the room even more when he passed me the mug.

"My dearest I am surprised you don't remember me? I am your husband. We have run away from good society and been living here with each other quite scandalously for years now. We are un-traditionalists and fell in love at first sight; even though I am royalty and you were a poor servant girl. I am really hurt you don't remember me. Here have a soothing cinnamon spice tea it will help with the healing. It is our favorite." He was so kind and attractive that I felt my heart race as he moved closer to me on the bed.

"I am sorry but I really do not remember even myself." I whispered as to not offend such a magnificent being as he was.

He felt familiar but strange and I knew I must have really hit my head hard if I couldn't remember this important and lovely man in my life.

"It is okay Guinevere I shall fill you in even though I feel you are always breaking my heart. We live happily in this humble cottage carved out of a giant redwood tree. We garden and harvest for food. Sometimes I take jobs hunting, and sometimes I play my flute and you dance in the market for coins. You are terrified of the lake since you drown when you were younger. But you swim when you are with me because you know I will always protect you. We live a peaceful quiet life away from the world and we have a pet wolf named Indigo. Look at yourself and try to remember our love, my pretty wife." The gorgeous elf's eyes sparkled with this purple magic in the sun's light.

I looked past him and the tub and saw the giant mirror along the wall. My reflection showed us both. There I was as I smiled with my perfect fangs and pale blue skin. We looked like a lovely pair of elves. Suddenly, I noticed both our hands clutching our mugs and frowned.

"Where has our wedding rings gone, if we are married? And what is your name and mine again, my dear?" I asked still saddened by the lack of gold on my finger and his.

I noticed my long golden braid that looked neat and tidy, and wondered if my darling husband braided my hair while I was sleeping. He smiled at me warmly and I knew he had taken care of me while I was ill which made me more at ease.

"My dear your name is Guinevere Graystar and my name is Treefer Graystar. You are my beloved, faithful wife. Actually our wedding day was tragic. The war is still going on between the humans and the elves. Humans had killed both our families and the devastation hurt us both. So we never even got to consummate our vows and marriage. Then you were bathing me and had your convenient accident. But I love you all the same and will wait for you whenever you are ready. We have our whole lives together now." He said but he certainly did not look like a Treefer, he was much too handsome for that name and it did not suit him.

Just now he said a little spell and held his closed palm up to me. Slowly he opened his palm and there inside were two matching golden rings. I placed my mug on the little wooden dresser beside the bed. There was elvish scribing written around both glittering golden bands as I picked up his bigger ring and placed it on his finger. Then he levitated his mug and slipped my small ring on my finger which fit perfect. I had become overcome with joy as I burst with excitement and hugged him as he froze; then hugged me back tenderly.

"Thank you Treefer for being so understanding this is so new to me. It is like there are no memories from before this moment of waking up in your presence." I said as I kissed his lips in gratitude and he kissed me back in an enchanting sweetness.

"It is okay my dear. We truly have the rest of our lives to get to know each other. I left hot water in the tub and your favorite dress and corset beside the bed. Please take your time and get dressed. I shall be in the garden. We have a huge day of work ahead of us." My husband said as he got up and left quickly.

I got out of bed and sluggishly discarded my nightgown. I slowly untied my long braid in the mirror. My pale blue skin seemed foreign but I felt beautiful as I looked at the sapphire necklace I had on. I stood there admiring myself trying to remember anything about being an elf. But no memories came to me as I stood there and admired myself in the mirror.

Suddenly, our front door swung open and my husband had announced that he had forgotten his straw hat. I heard his gasp but did not hide myself as he stood there with his mouth open. Why should I hide as he is my dear husband? I was brushing my long curly blonde hair and asked him to pass me the ribbon so I could braid my hair after my bath. He came over to me and as his hand touched my skin; I felt the electricity between us.

I felt the pull of my lips to his as I caught his hand and wrapped his arms around me. Our skin pressed together felt good as I kissed him with more passion and he kissed me back. His pale blue skin felt so amazing as I untied the leather of his loin cloth and heard him gasp again. His magnificence of splendor was massive and I held my breath as I felt his strong heart beating. His loving purple eyes looked deep inside my own and I felt his intense desire. I was leading him with kisses into the tub. I gently pulled him to me as I wrapped my legs around him when we sat in the warm water. His eyes opened into an intense purple glow as he looked at us together in the mirror.

"Guinevere I am rather soiled from the garden and we have so much work. Please my dearest...We need to get ready. Please join me in the garden my dear. There will always be time for intimacy and tenderness." He whispered sweetly as he trembled in kissing me and as my hands caressed him.

"I will wait for you when you are ready my darling husband. I believe our babies will be the most beautiful elves in the world and I want many." I whispered as I heard his breathless kisses.

He gently untangled my legs from around his torso while passionately kissing me still. Then he stood up and dried off using one of the linen he had brought for me. I teasingly stole his loose cloth as he was bent over trying to get some more linen for me to dry with.

"My darling wife we need to plant today so we have food for tomorrow. Even with magic I need the seed to grow before I can compel it to bring us a harvest." He said breathless in-between kisses as his hands held me tight and I embraced him now dripping on the floor.

"Yes my dear. Anything you say my sweet." I whispered as he kissed me so passionately I felt a little dizzy.

Then he kissed me but pulled away from gently embracing me and quickly grabbed his loin cloth off the floor. He walked softly towards the door and grabbed his straw hat as he left blowing me a kiss and a wink.

So I sauntered to the tub in a failed attempt to start having babies with the man who I was so clearly and passionately in love with. *He is right. We can't live off of love or can we?* I smiled at that thought and dreamed of my lavishing, handsome husband; and all the children we would have. While I quite happily bathed I sang a cheerful song and hoped he could hear me though the opened windows.

🌾🌾🌾🌾

CHAPTER 10

DORIAN

"What are you doing with the Princess, Dorian? You have always stayed on the right path until now." King Lucien whispered to me as I shrugged.

"It is harmless fun. I want her to know what it feels like to have nothing. I want her to know how I have lived all these past six years." I whispered sternly as I watched her in the garden working hard at digging holes to plant potatoes.

I knew she had been listening to me as I had shown her how to plant seedling potatoes and now she was planting a row. Meanwhile I was having a quick mug of mead with my goblin friend who looked distressed.

"I don't think this will end good Dorian. Besides that, what of her virtue? She will be a real outcast if her virtue is gone. And the King surely will shed the blood of the fiend that does it out of wedlock." My

King goblin friend whispered as he looked at Alora in sadness.

"I am not a monster Lucien. It has been the hardest thing in my life that I have ever had to endure. But I have been keeping her so busy with hard work she is too tired for anything else; just like a real housewife. I have also been complaining of my back and sleeping on the floor. It has been draining but I have been successful at thwarting her attacks of kisses at every moment she has flagged me. No, I barely even get close to her. Besides if I need anything in that sense I can just go to the widowed elf in the market. For a gold coin she will keep me plenty company. I don't need that spoilt Princess for anything except hard labor." I said as I chugged back my mead more aggressively.

"The widow has told me, you have never been her client. Seems like even the ogre shopkeepers haven't seen you in a month; but the dressmaking fairy has seen you plenty. Now; I don't like humans any more than you do Dorian. But even for the darkness in my soul, this isn't right. She is too pure to be around creatures like us. I heard in the market that the other girl that was impersonating the Princess was beheaded along with the knight. That Father of hers has always been a maniacal King in regards to his only Daughter and the heir to the throne. And now you have just given him fuel for his unquenchable fire of carnage against us magical creatures." Lucien shook his head as he looked at the trees.

"Relax, he will never find us. My wolf eats knights for breakfast. Indigo loves Alora with all his big puppy heart and would never let anything near her if he felt she was in danger. Besides, when she starts remembering I will bring her back and get the reward. It will be a win-win situation." I said and then chuckled.

"Maybe it will all work out. I can only hope for your sake my friend and Son of the forest. But what then if she never gets her memory back?"

"Yes, my friend. It will work out. But if her memory does not come back...Well I guess I shall marry her then for real and make her an honest woman. She won't be able to go home if she can't remember the King." I said and drank some more mead in merriment.

"Now we need to discuss business Dorian. The mountain lions are still killing my people. Please honor your promise it has been almost a month." Lucien whispered.

"Yes my friend, I will. I just have been so preoccupied scavenging for berries and nuts; and then tending to my gardens. I am sorry I forgot that my priority was to kill the lions. Don't worry my friend." I said just as I felt soft fingers gently caress the raised scars on my back.

I turned around and was surprised to see Alora smiling so pleasantly at me and my friend; that I blushed.

"My dearest husband, are you and King Lucien in need of some more mead to quench your thirst on this hot summer day?" She spoke so sweet my breath got stuck in my throat.

"No, we are well my dearest. Thank you for your consideration." I said as my eyes lingered in her pretty eyes.

"Is King Lucien going to bestow us with the pleasure of his company for dinner tonight? We always have room at our table for one more." She said even sweeter as she took my hand and kissed my ring finger.

"No my dearest, he has a whole loving kingdom to go home to. But thank you for the offering." I said breathless as her hands held mine and she looked even more ravishing in the dress I had purchased for her.

"My darling I need to do the laundry but I shall be back shortly." She whispered and then gently moved my head down so she could kiss my lips.

"Yes, there is no way this could end badly. Just remember who gave you those long lashes before I rescued you, dear Son of the trees."

Lucien said and chuckled before vanishing into the woods faster than I could blink.

"What would end badly my love?" She whispered in-between deep passionate kisses that made my heart start racing.

"Oh nothing my dear, we were just speaking a moment before of the mountain lion attacks." I said and lingered in her kisses and embrace.

"Yes my dear, those mountain lions have been so dreadful. I am so glad my strong husband will hunt them down." She whispered as she kissed me intensely sliding her hands down my muscular abs and I caught her hands before they had reached my massive hidden desire for her.

"My dear we have so much work to do today." I said as I kissed her but took a step back while still holding her loving hands.

"You are right my husband but I have been thinking a lot about how nice it would be to see our home full and happy. I am sure we could add a cradle beside the bed." She said as she whispered taking a step forward while undoing the top of the ribbons on her dress.

She was now placing my hands on her bountiful bosom and trapped me in more ravishing kisses. In her warm embrace I felt my loin cloth fall to the ground and her loving hands caressing my sacred soul.

"My heart is yours my husband for the taking." She said in-between kisses that stole my breath and made my whole body ache in yearning.

"I…I am sorry but I have to help King Lucien kill the mountain lions. Please be patient. I adore you but right now I have so many tasks at hand. Please do not wait for me for dinner, and please do not wait up for me as I will be home late." I said as my heart beat wild but I gently tied up her ribbons on her dress and covered her sweetness from the sun.

In more steamy kisses, I was successful at stepping away from her sensual trap and quickly re-attaching my loin cloth. Immediately, I turned away and whistled loudly for Indigo. The abnormally large wolf came prancing out of the woods where he had been hiding from the heat.

"Indigo, I need you to watch Alora when I am gone and guard her with your life." I said as the giant wolf nodded then licked my hand with his giant tongue.

"Alora? I have heard that name which you have called out many nights before in your sleep. Who is this woman? Am I not enough for you my handsome husband?" She said and I saw the heartbreak in her blue eyes which gave me agony in my gut.

"Guinevere she is you. We used to have cute nicknames for each other. You used to call me Dorian lovingly and I called you Alora." I said with a blush at her sweet puzzled expression.

"But why would we use different names?"

"Originally it was to hide from our enemies. Remember we were on the run? Now I only use it when I am completely and eternally in love with you." I said and it just came out.

I couldn't deny my heart anymore. This was the first time I had said out loud what I had been afraid to admit. My expression was still of concern; but now a radiance inside her made her glow. She was bursting with happiness like a candle had lit her up. She grabbed my hand and kissed my ring once more. Then she slowly walked away from me; only stopping to blow me a dreamy kiss. I stood there for another moment completely enchanted by her grace as her dress swayed on her hips and she juggled the basket down to the lake. I was tempted to run to her and carry the basket; but I knew if I followed her in that moment I might not ever leave.

I needed to breathe and went into the house. Now I trembled out of pure fear. *What have I done?* I looked around the house at how clean and sparkling it seemed. There were curtains now and the fresh roses I had picked for her were in a mug on the table. All of the quilts on the bed had been sewn. I had cut the wood but now it was stacked neatly beside the fireplace.

Everything was clean and tidy. She had made my little dump an actual home and prettier than it had ever looked. There weren't even any stacked dirty dishes in the sink. In just over a month, even though I had to teach her, she had made everything bright and new.

I gasped as I looked at the made bed. All this time I had slept on the floor, lying to her about my bad back. But the bed was always kept neat and tidy. Now it was missing something. On the floor beside my folded blanket was her pillow beside mine. *What am I to do now?* I silently wondered completely dumbfounded. She had infiltrated my bachelor life and became everything I had wished for in a soulmate and wife.

I stood there looking out the window as she stopped to play with Indigo. *Even my pet adores her. What will I do without her?*

Quickly I gathered my bow and satchel; packed full of deadly arrows. Then I left my lovely home and went down to the path that ran beside the lake where she was. I hoped I could be strong when I watched her gently jogging to meet me on the path.

"Keep safe Dorian, you have my heart with you. Here is some mead for you travels; I love you my husband. Hurry home soon with Godspeed and I shall pray for your safe return." She said as she passed me a leather flask and kissed me passionately with a tight embrace.

"Thank you Alora, I will travel with Godspeed. I love you so much Alora. See you shortly, my beautiful wife. I shall miss all of you while I am away." I said and lingered in her kisses and hug.

As I turned to walk away she grabbed my hand and kissed my ring. Then whispered; "I love you Dorian."

I immediately smiled back and answered; "I love you too Alora."

Then I made my way up the hill but I stood on the hillside watching her working hard on our laundry. My breath and a golden tear got caught as I watched her. I tried to gulp and couldn't. I stood there watching her work diligently and was just in silent awe of her grace. She had paused to dab the sweat from her brow and the sun had cascaded the gold of her braided hair on her shoulders. She was stunning. She was far from the awkward thirteen year old that I had saved all those years ago. She had always been the woman of my dreams. But I shook my head and turned away from her charm. She was still a human and the enemy. And in three days' time, with the full moon fast approaching, she will finally know the pain she has caused me. She will finally know the fear I bring to everyone who gets close to me.

🌾🌾🌾🌾

CHAPTER 11

ALORA

It was beautiful but terribly hot today. I finished hanging the laundry and then decided to go inside and have some of my darling husband's mead. *The name he always calls out in his sleep. It's from the reoccurring nightmare he has every night. I have heard him call out "Alora" quite often. But he only calls me "Alora" when he is eternally in love with me?* I thought as I had a lovely mug of mead followed by another mug.

Three mugs in, I started intensely dwelling on the name Alora as if uncontrollably attached. The name was so familiar to me and even more fitting than my own given birth name of Guinevere. *What is in this mead? Obviously I need to stop enjoying this homemade brew. It is so hot out though. The lake is right there and the heat is absurd. I just need more mead to conquer my fear inside me. I remember that I am afraid of the lake but I can't remember why? Grabbing another mug of mead was probably not the best idea considering my small frame but I need to cool off. And I need liquid courage for the lake.* I thought as I finished another mug and started preparing dinner for both of us. I knew my husband would be home late but I would still leave him a plate and light a candle for him before bed. The air was so muggy but I was grateful for the plentiful open windows of our home.

I quickly changed out of my hot dress and corset. I gathered the water for the bath to have a nice soak. Instantly, I felt better saturated in the tub and drinking my mead still. I had my thin lace nightgown laid out on the bed so that I would have something cooler to slip on after my bath. *What a wonderful day.* I thought as I gently closed my eyes.

🌾🌾🌾

CHAPTER 12

DORIAN

"I hit the creature straight in the chest. One arrow deep inside its ribcage and the monstrous mountain lion fled. How is beyond me! It must be a hell cat forged from the bowels of Hades himself." I shouted as I drank my posset at the tavern in the market.

"Dorian wounding the animal is good. But I need that killer gone. It has been devastating to my kingdom and you still haven't slain the beast or its mate. Both need to be gone before my kingdom suffers anymore." King Lucien said as he slowly drank his posset sitting beside me at the tavern.

"Can't you see it won't be long now my friend?" I said as I drank and ordered another.

"I think your heart is too focused on another task. The castle guards are in hoards everywhere now. You must get the lady back to the King or else it will be your head and the war will begin again. Not just from one side either. If your Father finds out you have been keeping a human in your house, you will have more trouble than if the humans capture you. Enough is enough Dorian. I heard the bluebird whistling in the forest; of a beautiful maiden that sings and dances in the woods while she forages for berries. She is too fine-looking and you cannot keep her there hidden for much longer." King Lucien said and sighed.

"I know okay. You are right. I have been trying to think of a spell to tell her the truth and fix her memory. I just don't know how. Right now I am her everything. I am her sun when she wakes and her moon while she sleeps. And for the first time in a very long time I'm not alone anymore." I admitted and then ordered another posset, as I had needed to get good and drunk to admit that truth.

"But you are living a lie Dorian. She is in love with you because she doesn't know the truth. What had started as a noble act of saving her life from the human-eating ogres has now become almost sinister and cruel. And you have never been this. You have not taken her virtue by consummating your fake marriage have you?" Lucien shouted.

"Hush down, someone will hear us my old friend. Of course I haven't, even though she has been treacherous in tempting me to give her children. I never knew being a husband was such a dangerous ambition. Besides if I were to take her virtue, I would be a villain." I said and belched loudly.

"This is villainous. Can't you see? She has family that is missing her." Lucien said with a frown.

"Ya well people go missing in the woods all the time. Besides I have no family and look at how wonderful I have turned out." I whispered back louder than I meant and some evil unicorns glared at me.

Lucien sat there with a deep frown and slowly shook his head. I knew he was completely right. Then he looked down at the brand new dress I had purchased for Alora, which was sticking out of my satchel and frowned even more deeply.

"I know okay. I know my friend you are right. I have to fix this. It is time that she knew the truth and was returned to her obnoxious Father." I said as I slammed one dirty gold coin on the bar to pay for all of our drinks.

Lucien gasped. But then our attention was drawn to a dark wizard in purple robes being kicked out of the tavern. The dark wizard's hat was pointy and his beard was longer than any beard I had seen in my life. His hair was whiter than snow and he was causing a commotion. The dark wizard had this crazy look in his eyes as he scanned the crowd stopping his gaze on me.

"I will show you the power of Hades. Tomorrow when the sun is high I shall make the moon rise to it, in a blood masterpiece. Take my heed, creature of the night." The dark wizard shouted as he pointed to me and then was kicked out of the tavern.

Lucien raised his eyebrows as I shrugged. The tavern was always filled with dark creatures that did dark bidding. It was generally a good time especially when the dancers came out. But weirdos came to the tavern a lot so I didn't care for what the dark wizard was saying. I knew when the blood moon was and it wasn't going to be during the high sun of the day. It was however, going to happen soon in two more nights after tonight.

"Your gold coin is soiled. You dug up your stash of gold for a rainy day didn't you?" Lucien said with his eyebrows raised.

"I may have, but do not worry my friend." I said and waved goodbye.

Then I left for the trail home back through the thick woods.

🌾🌾🌾🌾

I staggered into the house being as quiet as I could. I noticed the candle stub still lit for me. Then I looked over and seen the plate of berries, nuts and baked potatoes for dinner she had left for me. There was even a full mug of mead left out which I immediately pounded back.

Looking towards the bed I didn't see her though and my heart started racing to find her. I was shocked to find her passed out in the tub. She looked almost blue as I quickly pulled her out and started wrapping her with the quilt from the bed. I rubbed her arms and whispered for her to wake up.

She did slowly and then started kissing me. A wave of relief washed over me as I had gotten home in time before she froze to death. Ever so gently I helped slip the night gown over her head. Then I placed her in bed with the blankets covering her and brought her pillow back from the floor. I had an old chest against the wall which I had grabbed another blanket from and covered her again. She smiled at me and said goodnight as I whispered good night to her too. But then she grabbed my hand and pulled me down to her. She was passionately kissing me goodnight while gently holding me and I kissed her back.

Her kisses lingered on my lips even after she had closed her eyes in slumber. *Lucien never said it exactly but I know I am in a real mess. Hating her has completely backfired in my face. Now I am at a loss if I can even live without her.* I thought as I outstretched my blanket on the cold floor and let the silent golden tears flow. The house was so incredibly hot but even the heat wasn't bothering me as much as lying to Alora was.

I curled up into a ball and continued to silently let my golden tears soak my pillow. *I really have messed up this time. Only this time it was with someone I care about. No matter what the outcome I have to tell her the truth tomorrow morning; even though I will miss her.*

🌾🌾🌾

CHAPTER 13

ALORA

"Rise and shine my dashing husband. Dorian I made you coffee and breakfast. Please wake up, I wish to thank you for saving me from freezing to death in the tub last night." I said so sweetly as I couldn't stop looking at how handsome he was with the sunlight on him.

He was lying in the same spot on the floor for as long as I could remember; almost a full moon now. *That's my darling, such a gentleman even though I have wanted to rip his ragged loin cloth every day since I first saw him in it.*

"Yes my dear, I am up. I must have slept more sound than the dead. I don't even remember crawling to my floor bed. I have something of great importance to tell you. Just let me stretch; I am so weary." He said and stood up supernaturally fast.

I gasped as he stretched in the sunlight with his eyes closed and he was completely nude. He was in glorious monstrous form; attentively facing my direction as he yawned and then stretched like he was reaching to the heavens completely oblivious to my eyes. I held my breath but could not avert my delicate eyes from the most massive specimen of longing I had ever seen in my life that he always hid from me. *This is my gorgeous husband, the one I can't keep my hands or eyes off of.* I thought as I smiled so wickedly at him.

Then he stood there and yawned giving another quick stretch as he walked towards me with a puzzled expression. Then the breeze from the morning open window across his skin finally made him look down. He caught my expression and then quickly turned around. And then I became quite thrilled at seeing his muscular hind quarters that unfortunately was disappearing under his now attached loin cloth.

"I am so sorry Alora. I know you are not accustomed to that morning display. I hope I have not given you a fright. I remember it being so hot last night but I really can't recall taking off my loin cloth. Please forgive me. There really is something I must discuss with you and it is quite an urgent manner. Let us sit and have some of that delicious coffee." He spoke so sultry I nearly fainted by what I was going to tell him.

"I have a confession too my dear husband. You had retired to your floor and you were so sad last night. My heart heard your tears so I left my nightgown and brought my pillow down to the floor beside you. I comforted you all last night and we embraced until morning. I was so loving; and you were so open to my affections. Last night was the best night of my existence. We comforted each other sleeping in each other's arms." I boldly said as I reached and held his hand.

"You comforted me all last night?" He said and a shocked expression came over his face.

"Of course my husband; what kind of a wife would I be if I didn't go to you last night in your sorrow. I was sad because you were crying;

and saying over and over how you had messed up. You said that I was a Princess and I said to you of course I was. I had married you; a Prince for a husband. You had told me I deserved the palace life; and I said I deserve your love, always. I kissed away your sorrows in your wanting arms and you kissed me back. I have hungered for your love since the moment I can remember. I needed you last night just as much as you needed me. So I was the one that removed your loin cloth and my nightgown. I love you so much Dorian I couldn't stand to see you hurting and alone when I am your wife." I said as I kissed his hand while he held golden tears of sadness in his eyes.

"I have something else to tell you." His sultry voice held tenderness and I was glad he was okay with us comforting each other all night.

"I also know your secret. I hope you don't mind." I said and twirled in my new dress for him. My hair was braided and done up so pretty just the way he admired.

"You look so dazzling Alora. That shade of red is just so magmatic on you. I'm so glad you like it. It reminds me of the dress you wore when I had met you one day in the market." His deep voice was sultry and soothing as he drank almost all of his coffee in one gulp and then cleared his throat.

I watched as his breath got caught in his chest as he looked at me. I remember that same look many times on the faces of all the men in the castle courtyard. Then suddenly I became puzzled as I looked at Dorian. I ran past him in confusion and went to the mirror. I tried to feel my pointed elvish ears. My reflection was that of an elf but as I touched my skin on my ears there was no pointed tip.

"Dorian I haven't seen you since I was thirteen. I don't even know you. Why am I here and not in my kingdom? And what kind of treacherous sorcery has bewitched this mirror?" I demanded as I tapped my foot very unladylike.

"Please Alora come away from the mirror and I will explain everything. Please sit with me back at the table." He said in his deep soothing voice but then I heard him whisper an elvish incantation.

I watched in horror as my reflection in the mirror changed from elf back to human. I was myself again. I had blue eyes not purple eyes like his. I looked at my human teeth and human ears. Even my skin was now a golden tanned shade not pale blue. I was looking at myself and recognized every inch of my body. I watched in shock as the necklace itself changed from a sapphire back to the ruby. It was the same ruby missing from his golden crown upon his head. I remembered who I was and I was suddenly overwhelmed with emotion.

"You had me believing I was your wife. You had me believing we were poor outcasts, run off from good society. Dorian how could you?" I shouted as my tears flowed down my face and his golden tears were just as predominate as he stood up.

"Alora I have hated you since that very day I saved your life in the enchanted lake; since we were both thirteen. I was attacked at the lake and have been forevermore changed each month when the moon is full. You took that ruby and my life from me. I was banished and outcast all because I had helped the enemy; and worse I had become a half-breed. I was royalty and saving your life cost me everything. All because you had to swim and tease the darkness. But then you took my ruby. You kept a piece of me so I can never be whole. And the worst part is that you don't even care or know. You have carelessly flaunted my ruby around your neck like its glamorous powers could let you break all men's hearts without consequences." He said sternly and then cleared his throat as I stood there listening with both of our tears flowing down.

"You don't even know that all this time your powers of charm where because of that ruby. That ruby is a living piece of my heart that you have stolen all these years from me. So I have wanted revenge from the very first day I lost my family. I wanted you to feel the pain of going to bed hungry and working hard for your food. I wanted to show you what I have endured these past six years of loneliness because of you." His deep voice shook my heart but I still had no idea what he was talking about. He had never saved me.

"Here, take it then. I am sorry to have ever inconvenienced you. But I really do not know what you are talking about. You know what I think? I think you are a coward. You are hiding in the woods away from the war and the world. You can blame me all you want but can't you see how rich your life has been? You come and go as you please. You don't have to behave in public; nor have a million courtesans to please. You have a beautiful home and a roof over your head. And you know what? Since I have been here we have never went to bed hungry and I sure have never felt alone since being here with you. But all that doesn't matter Dorian. A true lady may not hate; but I definitely do not wish to ever be in your company again for what you have done. I hope you are happy with the knowledge that you have succeeded in every way of breaking my heart." I said as I took off the ruby necklace and placed it on the table with tears flowing.

Then I ran out the door. I didn't care where I was going I just didn't want to be around my fake best friend and my fake husband. My chest hurt so badly as I cried and ran. I had to stop and vomit along the path as I was so disgusted with Dorian. *I can't believe he actually made me care about him.* I thought as I wiped my mouth off using the bottom hem of my dress.

I was running and crying on a very worn path. It was dirty and it was littered with small pebbles which hurt my bare feet as I ran blindly. Suddenly I tripped and scrapped my knee tearing my lovely new dress. I sat down and cried harder with my face in my hands. I lifted my skirt to see the blood oozing out of the skin where a small rock was lodged. I screamed as I pulled the little rock out which hurt more than anything I had ever experienced. I moaned and cried as the blood flowed with my tears.

Then something with light brown fur caught my eye as it moved in front of me. Its yellow eyes were fixated on my knee; and then back and forth to my eyes in a cold unblinking game. The beast opened its jaw and I saw the bloody teeth were exposed in a sinister smile while looking at me. My scream remained caught in my throat just like I remained frozen in fear.

Without turning to see him, I witnessed from the corner of my eye, his large shadow standing with his bow and arrow aimed. I was still frozen but my tears were flowing.

"Don't move old hag or you are dead." His voice sounded more vicious than I had ever heard from him as he baited me.

"You know very well I am neither a hag nor much older than you are Dorian." I said with an air of snobbery.

"Good Lord you smell of the sweetest lilacs and seductive hormones Alora. Is that how you secretly seduced me and stole my heart?"

"How dare you speak to me that way Dorian. I am a lady." I shouted just as the giant mountain lion lunged for me.

An arrow went past my few stray curls and straight into the beasts exposed chest which had held another arrow. I sat there so still and shocked not able to move.

CHAPTER 14

DORIAN

The evil mountain lion remained still as it lay with its face in the dirt on the trail floor. I looked over to Alora's pretty tear streaked face now terrified. I could feel a small pain in my heart even though the ruby was now returned to my crown.

Suddenly Alora turned to me and her expression turned angrier than a leprechaun who had his gold stolen. She was just about to give me a good piece of her mind and I was going to take it when we both noticed the sky quickly darken. *Oh no the sorcery. Today the moon is rising in its full blood glory to meet the sun. Oh no, I can feel the change coming. Damn that wizard. I feel like tracking him down and biting his bloody head off.* I thought as I was forced to my knees from the erupting pain and screamed.

Alora's eyes went wide as she looked at me suffering. Meanwhile I was in excruciating pain and trying to discard my weapon and clothes along the trail. As I became hunched over clutching my stomach for dear life, a low growl came from behind me.

It seemed another mountain lion had been here with us, watching me slay its mate. I could see its massive shadow as it walked past me and moved slowly towards Alora. All I could do was scream from the agony, as I looked on in horror.

Meanwhile my back bones were breaking and stretching with my skin, longer and larger. I couldn't help but scream as my skin ripped apart and the black fur emerged as did my large black tail. I screamed again as my finger nails were being pushed out of my skin by razor sharp claws emerging from underneath; and my longer fingers were shredding the flesh, as fur the color of midnight ripped through my hands.

Now Alora was screaming as I watched on in anguish at the big cat which stalked closer and closer to her like she was a feast. I could see the long trail of saliva from the beast which made me worry even more. Then I screamed again which changed to a long howl as the rest of my teeth fell out of my gums and my fangs emerged. I howled again as the rest of my face ripped apart revealing the large red wolf eyes; large wolf nose; and giant black furred-tipped ears.

The darkness grew across the mountain path and in a blaze of light the sun and moon intercepted in a fire that made the skies red. The summer day had turned to night; and the blue skies had been replaced with an ominous blood moon shine. It reminded me of the blood I needed and could not be denied. I was transformed completely and looking for vengeance as I carried that hate from the dark wizard in my wolf form.

The big cat managed to try to swipe at Alora and missed her just before it realized what a mistake it had made by turning its back on me. I immediately sank my fangs in it and drank the luscious blood like water. But I didn't finish it as I saw Alora screaming. Instead I picked up the beast and threw it hard against the mountainside.

Then I bent down to check to see if Alora was okay.

"Get away from me you monster." She shouted at me and started throwing rocks in my direction.

I would be lying to myself if I said that didn't hurt. But it didn't hurt as much as the fangs and claws that just sank into my shoulder. The mountain lion had caught me off guard and made me disorientated as I wrestled with the beast while Alora screamed.

Then, my thirst took over uncontrollably as I opened my jaws wider and had the lion's throat in my grasp. I sank my fangs in so deep I heard the beast's larynx pop and I drank. This was the blood that would soothe me. It was the life force I depended on each month. As I drank the blood I watched Alora's pretty face change from fear to what I imagined was a look of disgust; and I turned from her as I finished the beast off. She didn't know what it felt like to be cursed. I needed the blood I could not help it.

Suddenly I felt dizzy as I placed my large werewolf paw to my head where my left long wolf ear was. There was a lot of my blood loss as I felt the pain from the gash the big cat must have gotten in. The dizzy feeling became worse as the night was turning back to the normal day hours of light. *I feel so weak now.* I thought just before being brought back to my knees in pain returning to the woodland elf-form I was born.

My pale blue elvish hand turned to reach for Alora in a plea to her heart but no words came from my lips as the darkness was starting to overtake me.

🌱🌱🌱🌱

CHAPTER 15

ALORA

"Dorian you are nothing more than a monster. You deserve to be left here for dead after the treachery you have bestowed on me." I shouted but looked at how still his form was.

His gentle hand outreached for mine in a weak helpless movement. But my heart still hurt and beat fierce. His betrayal wounded my very soul even though he had just saved my life. I could not forgive him.

My skin crawled as I moved towards his bloodied body surrounded by the dead creatures by his side. There were chunks of black fur and brown fur everywhere. I looked onto the handsome elf I had been so attracted and charmed by in the last month. Suddenly, I picked up a large rock and walked over to where he was lying on his side where his eyes were closed.

As I hovered over him, his purple eyes fluttered to me holding the giant rock over his head. My eyes burned with hatred as I threw down my rock hard as it made contact. Dorian's eyes were a peaceful purple as we both listened to the sickening thud when the rock connected to the mountain lion that had stirred. Now the beast was finished.

I immediately dropped to my knees and vomited to the side of the beast lying beside Dorian. *I can't be here. I will be disgraced from the royal life I deserve to be in. I will be ruined if I stay.* I thought as I wiped my face off the bottom hem of my beautiful dress which was torn. I knew I hated Dorian and returned to burning my angered stare into his peaceful wounded eyes.

Then I heard his faint exhale with no next inhale.

"Dorian? Dorian wake up." I shouted as I moved to his lifeless body where blood was oozing from the mountain lions chew marks on his muscular torso.

He wasn't breathing and so I worked hard at giving him the kiss of life and breathing air back into his lifeless body.

🌾🌾🌾

CHAPTER 16

DORIAN

Gasping, I awoke and painfully tried to sit up.

"Dorian if you move your stitches will be torn out again and I can promise you I will not be as compassionate sewing your flesh a third time." I heard Alora's cold voice and looked over to see her at our table drinking a tea.

She got up and brought me a mug of tea as I gazed into her steel blue eyes. I noticed my wedding ring was on the table beside hers. I then looked down at the claw marks as she handed me the mug and then returned to the table. I gasped as the teeth and claw marks started from my shoulder and ended somewhere below the navel. I moved the blanket frantically and sighed as my manhood was still glorious and intact. I exhaled out of relief and quickly moved the blanket back as I looked for my clothes that were bedside the bed.

I looked over to Alora who wasn't paying attention to me as she gazed at the swans on the lake. She had this displeasing look across her face as she sat in front of a giant satchel of gold coins on the table. It hurt me to even see her unhappiness.

"Why didn't you leave me wife…I mean Alora?" I stammered out and coughed.

"Don't call me that ever again Dorian. I almost left you there; you being that big hairy pathetic excuse for a werewolf. I almost left you for dead. But I gave you the kiss of life and brought you back. I don't know why I am here now. King Lucien stopped by to check on you and dropped off your reward for killing both mountain lions. He was so grateful he gave you another satchel of gold coins of which I hid in your cookie jar for a rainy day. But now that you are up and alive I want you to know I am going home. I don't care if I get lost on the way. I can't be in this home anymore with you. The two days you took to recover was enough." Alora said in a hushed but aggressive tone as she stood up gracefully.

I noticed her hair was properly braided and only lacked the gold that a month ago sat upon her proud temple. She looked at me so fierce I felt daggers in my most precious muscle that she stung. I quickly attached my loin cloth and slipped my shirt over my head and then tried to slip on my pants in agony.

"I will show you the way." I said as I took a big drink of my favorite sweet tea she had made me.

"I don't want you to Dorian. I want nothing from you ever again. Congratulations on your revenge of my wounded heart. I will be lucky if I am not shunned and disowned. I am grateful the doctor will lie to the King about my virtue though and spare me the gallows. I would blame you if I could. I am lucky that my new boring husband will not care as long as I am his reward of my kingdom." She said as she had tears streaming down her cheeks but still looked at me with daggers in her eyes.

"Do you even know I would have cherished your lips to mine, not even a trio of days past. I gave you the kiss of life to bring you back to the world of the living. I should have let Hades take you. Your lips certainly were that frozen before I decided I was a true lady and wasn't going to let you die." Alora shouted now and cried while running out the door just as I got up.

My side was bleeding again but I knew I would heal. I just needed more time. So, I supernaturally wrapped it with linen and then grabbed my bow and satchel full of arrows. I also grabbed our wedding rings and stuffed them in my pocket. I whistled loudly but Indigo did not come. He was gone, just as she was. I chased after her in agony as she stormed the wrong path.

"Alora this path will take you to my kingdom. Please do not go down this path. I implore your heart to turn around." I pleaded with her as she stopped and turned to me with an angry glare.

"I think I will go to your kingdom and tell your Father about your recent exploits. I'm sure he would love to hear about your deception." Alora said with tears still streaming down her face.

"You wouldn't even get to the gate of the kingdom Alora. This path is that treacherous and I cannot protect someone whose pigheadedness will get us killed." I said sternly now and I could feel the combination of pain and anger heating my eyes in hers.

"How dare you speak to me that way Dorian." Alora said as she walked back to me and raised her hand but I gently grabbed her hand before she could.

"Can we please call a truce? Let me get you back to your castle before we both get killed for losing our tempers on each other." I said so deep I watched her surprised eyes as I held her hand more gentle than I believed ever possible.

"I agree only because I truly believe that my Father will hunt you down and slay you like the dog you are. How dare you keep me as a prisoner for this past month." She said in a breathless whisper as her eyes travelled down my body to my bloody bandages on my side.

I gently held her soft ring-less hand on my open palm not even in a grip and she did not move from my hard callouses. Her cool eyes even lingered back from my painful wound to my hard stare. Humans were treacherous lustful creatures and she was no exception. Her bountiful curves and soft skin betrayed my senses every time I gazed upon her. I hated myself for my treachery but disliked myself even more for being enchanted by her absolute loveliness.

"Let's go back to the other path." I said and then she took her hand back greedily as if my skin was poison.

I lead the way down another path less travelled. It was so less travelled it had been overgrown.

"We are leaving late in the day Princess and we will have to make camp half-way." I said and continued to walk forward.

"But you travel back and forth to the market daily." She called out from behind me.

I stopped to take her hand as we carefully crossed the large creek and she held my hand tight.

"I always leave at dawn and can be back before dusk if I run and am in good health. But we are leaving so late in the afternoon we will have to stop to make camp. Some parts of the forest are not safe at night when the moon is high and we won't be able to just travel through." I gravely said as I looked at the sun setting.

"But I wish to go home quickly Dorian." She stated but continued to walk behind me.

"I wish you home just as quickly. But even I cannot save you from some evils that dwell in the darkness." I said and kept walking forward.

"You could barely save me in the light of day. I swear Dorian, I have been rescued and that by far was the worst rescuing I have ever experienced. And I have been courted by hundreds of Princes much more handsome than you." She said as she took my hand and I helped over some jagged rocks that were on the path.

"I bet you have Princess." I muttered under my breath as I smiled while helping her again.

That was the last of her rants as we moved through the thick bracken overgrown on the path. My bare feet were sore and I stopped only for a moment when some lush green grass grew on the side on the dirt path.

I didn't know why but the closer we got to her castle, the more I felt better and better. There were no more lies between us. There were no spells draining my energy to make her look like an elf in our mirror; or any reflective surfaces. I would be finally free of her and this horrible last month. I tried to hide my happiness and placed a huge scowl on my face as we tread the pathway to freedom.

🌱🌱🌱

CHAPTER 17

ALORA

The mere sight of Dorian's frown gave me immense pleasure. I wanted him to miss me and I couldn't wait to be rid of him. Dorian stopped so abruptly I ran into his back. Being that close I smelt the scent of the woods and berries off his skin and tried to close my memories of his heart so close to mine.

Then I saw it. The reason he had stopped. The giant black furred creature up ahead looked barely moving.

"Oh Indigo, what have they done to you?" Dorian cried out and ran over to the large wolf that was whimpering.

I ran over too and gasped as I noticed the two arrows sticking into Indigo's ribcage. The arrows each held a royal red ribbon from my kingdom and I gasped at the ignorance of my guards. What did my kingdom do? They aimed their arrows at the biggest most kindest of creatures, all because of his fierce appearance.

I dropped to my knees beside Dorian. Dorian held Indigo so gingerly almost like he was cradling the wolf's head in his arms. He was whispering in faint loving murmurs to the wolf in some elvish language and my tears started flowing. I looked at what surrounded the giant wolf and gasped at the massive bloodshed.

I tried to listen to the sweet hums of love coming from Dorian's lips to his pet wolf. Then I noticed the same ruby from my old necklace back in his crown and glowing.

"Indigo you have to hold on my friend. I love you. Please stay with me. The magic will work if you just can live after I pull the arrows out. Hush now my sweet." Dorian's proud face was drenched in golden tears as he helped his friend.

My tears seemed to have an endless supply as I picked up the great black paw and petted it softly. Indigo was panting as he was struggling in the biggest fight of his life. I watched Dorian gently pulling out one of the arrows and gasped as I saw the arrowhead saturated in Indigo's deep crimson richness of life.

Then I held my breath as the other arrow was pulled out intact. An eruption of blood started flowing from both holes and matted the already wet black fur.

Dorian quickly placed his hands to stop the bleeding while he chanted a spell. His hands were glowing as he continued to keep them pressed on both wounds.

Then I could not hide my shocked expression as the same ruby I had held onto in glamor broke out of Dorian's crown and floated down in hovering inches above his bloody hands. The ruby looked like it was radiant in the light as it waited while Dorian opened his hands. Then the ruby buried itself inside the giant wolf's side through one of the open wounds. There was a sudden flash of purple mist that sparked so bright I had to flinch and had to shield my eyes with my arm.

My breath escaped me and I felt my heart skip a beat as I watched the magic glowing and sealing the wound instantly. Before my eyes I had witnessed the wound completely being healed. The giant wolf got up whimpering as it jumped on Dorian and licked his face over and over.

The giant wolf was crying to Dorian and even gave me a few licks as I giggled in pure happiness.

"Yes I love you too my brother wolf, my best friend. I couldn't live without you either." Dorian said and then cried golden tears as he hugged the large animal.

Indigo looked like he was hugging Dorian back as he rested his large head on Dorian's shoulders.

My eyes were filled with pure joy and suddenly I realized I had never felt this overwhelming feeling of love before. I had never had anyone that had treasured me enough to save my life with the magic of love.

🌾🌾🌾🌾

CHAPTER 18

DORIAN

I couldn't stop my happy golden waterworks as Indigo kept licking my face. My best friend was alive and healed. It was a tricky magic but it had worked a second time in my life. Indigo was so happy he bounded me and I laughed as we rolled on the grass. The giant wolf rushed over and licked Alora's pretty face. Her smile was so warm and loving. She did not hide from all the affection Indigo was giving her and my heart swooned from the happiness.

"Dorian I'm filled with so much joy. I am almost in rapture at your abilities." Alora said and I couldn't help but smile at her wet face that matched mine.

I wasn't pleased that she had been crying but I was pleased at the fact she cared for Indigo too. And if she was moved to weeping for my best friend in the whole world then maybe the Princess still had a beating heart in her cold exterior.

"Come Indigo, we must travel a little further up into the dark woods and then we must part my Brother Wolf. I can't risk you getting too close to the kingdom again." I called to Indigo as he wagged his tail and then ran up ahead of us as a scout.

"How did you know the arrows were from my kingdom?" She softly asked.

"I have been hunted and captured by your guards. I have been chased by your archers' arrows for many years. The quills hold your kingdoms royal red ribbons." I said as I extended my hand to help her over some rough terrain and she took it without hesitation.

"Why would my kingdom be chasing you Dorian? Why would they even be on the lookout for you, other than the war that is?" She asked as she let me place my hands on her waist to lift her over a very jagged rock and then we continued down the path.

"They were after me ever since the beginning. Your Father knew and hated the fact that a woodland elf had saved his Daughter's life. And he knew I had two more heart rubies in my crown that were just as magical as the one I had gifted you." I spoke more frank than I should have but I did not realize this until she stopped abruptly.

I turned around to see her shocked expression and had no idea why she wasn't moving forward when she knew nightfall was upon us. We needed to find the large old oak for refuge.

"What do you mean Dorian? You keep saying that you saved my life but I have no recollection of this. You never saved my life. I met you and then left you in the forest that one day when I was thirteen." Alora spoke and my mouth gaped open.

"Let us be logical, shall we Princess? You just witnessed me use my magic to bring Indigo back to life with one of my heart centered rubies. If you had my other heart ruby then logically I would have saved your life as well." I said as I extended my hand and she took it as I was leading her into the forest.

"But you saved Indigo because you loved him. We hadn't even known each other for mere hours that day." She said still puzzled.

"Yes my Princess it was mere hours. But do you honestly believe you just happened to have my heart ruby by chance?" I asked her sweetly as I warmly smiled at her still trying to piece everything together.

"No but I don't understand Dorian. I don't remember anything except our meeting. I was very sick after that trip to the woods and that was why my Father never brought me back." She said and looked at the meadow still puzzled.

"Alora do you trust me?" I asked her.

"A lot has happened Dorian." She said and looked into my eyes.

"Do you trust me?" I asked her again as I was looking deeply into her soft blue irises.

"Yes, I guess I do." No more than she said the words I stepped over to where she stood.

In one smooth motion I whispered an elvish incantation as I placed my hands on the sides of her face. I gently cupped her cheeks as I kissed her forehead while my hands glowed and then I kissed her with all the passion in my soul. I knew my love could heal her memories.

🌾🌾🌾🌾

CHAPTER 19

ALORA

"Dorian I remember." I gasped as the flood of memories came back to me, including us together forbiddenly in the alleyway. *All this time, the mysterious handsome stranger that I made love to in the alleyway was in actual fact Dorian. No wonder I was so drawn to him that day.* I thought as I looked into Dorian's sweet purple eyes.

"I remember everything. I remember us singing together. Your voice is so magical it stirred my soul. I remember us having fun swimming in the lake and then...Dorian...I remember you warning me and I didn't listen. Oh Dorian, I remember the darkness grabbing me and you fighting the beast that was dragging us to the bottom of the lake. I should have listened to you. I remember and I know I died that day. You really brought life back to my body." I said and cried as he immediately embraced me.

"It's okay Alora you are safe now. You will always be under my protection. I will never let anything ever hurt you again." His deep voice soothed my soul and I realized the ruby wasn't our only connection.

I stayed in his arms while my mind raced through dark thoughts and mixed feelings. I was trying to piece together the entire puzzle of why somethings in my life had never made sense. Including why no other male had I ever desired or been magnetically drawn to.

"That means my Father lied to me." I said in utter sadness at the fact that my Father might actually be more villainous than I had ever dreamt.

"Oh Dorian, I remember seeing the changeling bite you when we were in the abyss of darkness before I drown. I remember the teeth marks sunken into your torn blue skin. So the creature cast you to be a werewolf?" I asked in remembering him change.

"It forever altered my whole form Alora. I will live forever; and hundreds of years past my Father and even generations of my kingdom. I am the dark creature of freedom that my soul longed to be. I am the Alpha of the pack and brethren to all wolves now. The darkness gave me more power but changed me to the very secret thing I held deep in my heart. It was my secret of secrets. I have never shared the story I am going to share with you with anyone. But I know my heart and all of its forbidden desires. One day I had been wandering the woods looking for deer to hunt and had found this abandoned wolf pup. In the ancient ways of my kingdom of woodland elves; I was raised to kill such a thing. The woodland elves believe it was kinder to kill the baby than let it grow up in this cruel world motherless." He deeply said and cleared his throat as the meadow grew eerily quiet.

"The moment I looked into his darling yellow eyes I knew I could not harm him. I adopted Indigo and was secretly raising him; even sneaking him into my bed chamber at night through the hidden passageways in my castle. How could I kill such a small but magnificent creature that was just as lonely as my heart had been? Immediately, I loved him like he was my own brother and kept his health and spirits up. But the thing about the darkness is it always knows your hearts desires. Now I am cursed and forced to change every full moon. I am a hybrid and an outcast to my family thrice over." His deep voice enchanted me as I listened in awe.

"Why thrice over Dorian?" I asked as I embraced him tight.

"It was thrice that I had disobeyed my Father. Once was for not slaying the wolf pup. Twice was when I had been bitten and instantly became a hybrid and beast. Thrice was when I had saved a human girl from drowning and fell in love with her the very first moment I saw her blue eyes." His sultry voice had mesmerized me as I stayed in his arms and he kissed my forehead.

"So that was why I had your heart ruby?" I asked as the air got caught in my throat.

"Yes Alora. And I blamed you for everything that went wrong in my life since; including when my heart fell in love with yours in the market alley. I am so sorry Alora. I was an idiot and should not have deceived you. I will be bringing you back to your kingdom tomorrow by noon. I promise to keep you protected and keep you safe as we journey to your castle. Then I will never see you again after I have delivered you home." Dorian whispered and kissed the top of my head once more as I just closed my eyes and stayed in his strong arms.

"I can't believe my Father lied to me. He always spoke about how evil the woodland elves are. Our kingdom has been at war with your kingdom ever since. In fact, our entire kingdom is convinced woodland elves eat humans. Can you believe that?" I said still in astonishment.

"I'm sure Alora he was only trying to protect you for your own good. But for the record, woodland elves have never eaten humans; that has always been ogres. The general store of which you and your friend stumbled into was an ogre's store. You really were knocked unconscious but from your own knight that wanted to rush you and only you home; to be engaged. You had been left because of the color of your cloak. If I had not brought you to my home you would have ended up on the ogre's dinner menu that night." He calmly spoke as I shuddered.

"But what of the accords and the Peace Treaty which clearly states that if humans are captured that we are not to be eaten?" I asked.

"The ogre shop keeper, named Treefer, was going to break the Treaty and eat you both anyways. He was arguing with his wife as you stumbled in and was still distracted by the argument as I left with you. The Peace Treaty also states that prisoners are not to be harmed if captured in the war. But I have witnessed many innocent victims captured from your kingdom." He said and looked deep into my alarmed eyes which soothed me briefly.

"Dorian I now know the truth. I know your heart and my forgotten memories, but I still feel betrayed. I don't know if I can trust you ever again. It hurts my soul to think about our fake life together and how happy we were. And it hurts my soul knowing our future happiness that could have been." I said but absent mindedly stayed in his eyes and his arms.

"I am truly sorry Alora, if I could declare a mild case of temporary delirium I would. If I could weave a spell to turn back the clock of time I would. But even the grandest of sorcerer's cannot change what has passed. There is only today, tomorrow, and the rest of our lives. But there is always a chance for me to hope, dream, and do better. So the next time I won't hurt the one I love with what is left of my wretched heart." His deep voice was rich with sorrow as he gave me a tiny squeeze.

Somehow we had been levitating through the woods as he was

holding me and then we had stopped in front of a giant oak tree. He gently lowered our bare feet to the soft grass in front of the massive tree's trunk.

As we stood in front of the tree he drew an invisible symbol on the bark with his glowing finger. Afterwards he stood there and knocked three times and a large door appeared before us in the tree's rough, gray bark. The seams were glowing as the door creaked open.

"Here we are. This is our shelter for tonight. We shall be safe here. I have lots of blankets and there is a nest of dried ferns." He spoke as his spirits lifted when we had viewed the tiny room.

"Dorian what is this place?" I asked as this little space was much smaller than our cottage home had been by the lake.

"This is my first home from when I was banished. This is the exact forest we sang and skipped in. This is also where I raised Indigo. It's our wolf den." Dorian said quite happy as he extended his hand and I took it while stepping inside the tree home.

This little home was very similar to his new home, but it was much smaller. There wasn't room for a tub; a raised bed; or a kitchen. There was a little fireplace with a kettle however; and then there was a soft bed on the floor made of ferns. This place only held one large window high up in the tree as if to see the stars at nighttime. But right now the window had streaked the most vivid pinks, oranges, and blues as the sun was setting in the glorious sky above. The sun's brightness had made such a striking light show inside the tree and I sat down in amazement.

But I looked over to Dorian as he was getting blankets out and was worried. I couldn't help but feel strange now. I had seen the truth and he had confessed so much. But I was still having a hard time letting go and trusting him again. *How can anyone love anyone at first sight? Yet I know he did. I watched him save Indigo with the same love magic.* I thought as he looked over to me and I blushed.

I had so many mixed feelings about Dorian. But my heart couldn't stop the deep longing for him. All I wanted was to be in his loving presence and strong arms. I was completely confused about that because he really had betrayed me in the worst way. But I also knew a secret hidden deep inside my heart.

I watched him starting a little fire in stone fireplace. He smiled over to me as he used his magic and placed the spices in our mugs. When his eyes met mine again I blushed as he caught me looking at him waiting for the copper kettle to boil. The big secret of my fragile soul was that I did not have a piece of his heart anymore but he definitely had a piece of my heart.

🌾🌾🌾🌾

CHAPTER 20

DORIAN

"Princess you will be safe here tonight. You must be well rested for your journey tomorrow. It will be a very long day. But I need you to promise me tonight you will not leave the protection of the tree. You must not leave this space of comfort under any circumstance. Tonight the moon will be blood red and completely full. My soul will be calling to run and hunt with Indigo and the others hiding in the forest. Please do not leave the safety of the giant oak. When I change to the wolf sometimes I lose my senses and most times I follow my wild heart. Please do not become my next meal. I need blood to satisfy the beast's primal urges. Listen to my words and take heed Alora; stay here where it is safe." My voice was much deeper than intended but I hoped she was listening.

As she nodded her head she seemed more absent-minded and in a daydream or fantasy. I started to second guess myself if she was just looking at my magmatic eyes again. *Damn alluring elf eyes. The shade is a systematic charm of human ladies being unable to resist the magic.* I thought as I smiled back but worried about her.

I had already hurt her and I did not wish to hurt her again. It was ironic how I was from the dark woodland elf clan and we were not evil. I think we had adopted the term *'dark'* just so predators and other monsters would leave us alone.

I had gotten out one of my long shirts that she could use for the night and left it on a blanket for her. With disregard for me watching, she started undressing quickly in front of me before I could pass her to leave the tree to give her privacy. I wondered if it was her royal upbringing with servants dressing and undressing her that helped her discard her corset and overdress fast; or if it was because our fake life was so real that she couldn't help dressing in front of me still. Either way I left the tree just in time as I caught her enchanting smile.

Unfortunately in my haste I left my bow and satchel full of arrows resting just inside the door. So I decided to take a little stroll and see if there were any ripe fruit left on the gooseberry bushes. To my stars there were. I picked a plethora of berries and then walnuts for our dinner using my shirt as a basket.

I was so happy with my forage that I entered the tree in haste and became breathless at the sight of Alora. *Why does she tempt me so? I don't think it out of cruelness but she must like the attention. She smiles every time as if she wanted to*...My thought trailed off as I almost dropped our dinner.

I saw her unbraided hair which was cascading golden curls over my shirt she was wearing. She was too bewitching for words as I stood there and had to clear my throat as I knew I was finding it hard to swallow.

"Alora I brought us some dinner." I spoke and cringed at the frog in my voice as I tried to clear my throat.

"Thank you Dorian, I feel so hungry after our journey. I am so parched as well. It is unfortunate that we don't have some of that good mead right now. I sure could use it before I face my Father tomorrow." She said and sighed as I sat beside her and we ate.

"Well I do have several jugs here Alora, but do you think that is wise after all we need to get up early tomorrow." I said as I tapped the wall across from the fireplace.

Instantly, a cupboard opened up with three jugs filled of mead and two pottery mugs. Alora's smile became wider as she looked at me and drank her tea in haste.

"Dorian what could possibly go wrong with that little bit of mead. I don't think it could hurt us to have a drink." She said sweetly as she grabbed a jug mischievously.

"You are right Alora, what could it hurt but to have only one?" I said as uncorked the first large jug that she had passed me.

🌿🌿🌿🌿

Four drinks later and we lay with our shoulders touching each other's on the soft floor of ferns. We were enjoying ourselves as we drank. We were watching the shadows of clouds on the walls and all the amazing colors of a sunset painted in the ceiling window.

We had been speaking candid of life; and the pain and blessings of friendships. I had just finished telling Alora of the time I had caught two toads making out and one vomited green ooze all over the other. Her merriment was the best music to my ears. I relished in hearing her laughter it hadn't been that long, but felt like forever since her smile could be heard in her voice.

The sun was slowly setting as she spoke about the servants being friends with her even though it wasn't allowed. She mentioned that she and some servant named Elizabeth were always getting into trouble. They would get into the royal stash of different types of barley ales and meads at the castle. Sometimes they would accidently catch the scullery maid with the baker smooching up a storm. I laughed at her descriptions of the funny humans who thought they were clever with a secret romance that everyone, including the King, knew about. We both seemed to laugh and laugh as the sun hung low in the sky.

With one more mug of mead my flute came out of the cupboard and I played for her the same meadow sentimental song from when we were kids. She surprised me as she sang with me while the flute played with magic. Our voices seemed to hold magic as I closed my eyes to the lovely melody. I turned to face her adoring eyes as I smiled compassionately and then suddenly are faces were close as she lay on her side. Somehow we were much closer than before as she giggled and kissed my cheek and I closed my eyes as my heart fluttered. Then she giggled and kissed my forehead as I closed my eyes each time with her kisses getting more frequent and closer to my lips.

Her hands went to my face and I felt her tongue push open my mouth. But this time I longed to feel her tongue stroking mine. I had been missing her before she had left. And even though my ribcage wound was barely healed, I needed her warmth.

It was as if a wave of emotions flooded over us as we kissed and held each other in soft whispers of love. Everything was moving in a sweet feverish rhythm without logic; just our massive hearts exploding with passionate cries. *I am so in love with you Alora.*

Then she lay on me as I held her tight. I could feel her heart beating rapidly against my chest that thundered in a breathless happy mess. It had been such a long day and I relished in holding her as we fell asleep. *I just need a little nap in loves arms before the full blood moons kisses.*

Just a moment of bliss and the sweetness from Alora's love before the curse will claim me tonight. I thought as I shut my eyes. I was so completely in love and so full of contentment that I completely forgot all my worries and sadness that awaited us tomorrow. Our chests fell and rose together in the sweetness of slumber and I felt complete for the first time in six years.

🌾🌾🌾🌾

CHAPTER 21

ALORA

When Dorian played his flute with his magic so he could sing to me; that's when I knew my heart had fallen for him all over again. I couldn't help how dashing he had looked shirtless and in his loin cloth as we lay there just moments before laughing about the strangest of friendships. He had just melted me. I sang with him and our voices seemed heavenly.

Even though I knew it was wrong, I giggled as I started kissing him and he closed his eyes each time. He let me have my loving way with him. Then he gave me back all the immense fire of desire I knew he still had for me that matched my own fiery passion for him.

Afterwards, I lay on his chest exhausted and deliriously happy while my golden curls draped over him and my body clung to his. I was in his arms and I just knew; I wanted his arms around me for the rest of my life. I never wanted to let go of Dorian. He was perfect.

Tomorrow I was going to beg my Father to let me marry Dorian. If my Father said no; well I was just going to run away with Dorian anyways. I don't think I could ever be without him. *I love you Dorian.* I tried to say but fell asleep fast, listening to his strong warrior heart beat. The smell of the berries and forest off his skin; was like the familiar scent of a cozy blanket I just wanted to always be wrapped in.

🌿🌿🌿🌿

Later I felt Dorian shift underneath me and then there was only a chill where he was just lying beside me. I immediately sat up as I heard the giant oak door click shut.

"Dorian." I whispered as I threw on his long shirt he had given me.

My mind was racing about all the guilt I suddenly had that had just come back to the surface as the mead had made me a little tipsy. *The darkness had taken a bite out of him instead of me. This is my entire fault that he is forevermore changed. All because I thought it would be fun to prove him wrong and swim where I should not have. And if Dorian wouldn't have saved me from the creature then this would be my life or worse. My Father hated the magical communities so much that I bet I would have been beheaded and then burned. I had even drowned that day that Dorian had saved me again. What right do I have to stay privileged while my dearest friend and lover suffers alone as an outcast?* These thoughts burned my unrest as I got up and chased after him in his long shirt.

Tonight the full moon was blood red as it hung high in the sky giving the forest this sinister look. Everything matched the crimson hue lighting the way of where Dorian seemed to be fleeing for his life.

Without thought I continued to run after him, onto this worn out path that it seemed like hundreds of feet or paws had travelled carving their way through the grass. I didn't even stop as he let out this horrific scream. *Dorian please stop running. I am here for you. You aren't alone my dearest friend.* I thought as I kept following him.

We had run to the clearing by the lake. This was the same enchanted lake that I was terrified of. I had just realized this as I watched Dorian drop to his knees and clutch his stomach as he bent over so low his forehead touched the ground. He then screamed so terrible that a chill ran down my back and I froze no more than ten feet away from behind him.

"Go now Alora before it is too late. I don't know if I can control my thirst for blood and I have to feed the beast tonight." Dorian spoke breathlessly as he panted and then suddenly screamed again as he clutched his ears.

I gasped as I watched his skin shred with the large black furry wolf ears that emerged.

"I cannot leave you Dorian. You shouldn't be alone right now or ever again." I said as he turned his head to look at me and I saw the pain and sorrow in his eyes.

"You must…You must leave me Alora. Tonight especially, there is blood on the full moon. If I bite you, even in accident, you will forever be changed by that moon Alora. I would never curse anyone like this. It burns my soul. The freedom of the wild has to rip itself out of my elven flesh. The freedom of my soul needs to run and howl. The price is blood Alora. I need to feed on blood. Please go now before tis' too late." He shouted and then screamed clutching his stomach.

"Dorian I was happy being adored and fabulously rich. I was content to read my bedtime fairytales. I had never known that real magic existed. I had never known that real love could beat through my pampered golden heart. I never knew I wanted to be in a fairytale of real magic and real woe. If I leave you to suffer it will break my heart as well. We are connected and I'm not leaving you Dorian. I'm...I'm so madly in love with you. You have been the best thing that has ever happened to me. And I would not trade our friendship for all the golden thrones in the world. My heart cannot let you go because you are my happily ever after. I love you Dorian with all my mind, heart and soul." I spoke as my tears come down from admitting the truth and I touched his bare back which felt on fire.

"Please Alora I beg of you. I could not bear it if something happened to you. The others will be coming out soon because I am there leader and now the King of the werewolves. There are many others from my Fathers kingdom and they are all outcasts like me." Dorian clutched his stomach and screamed again.

"There are others?" I asked completely oblivious up until now that there was a possibility of more werewolves running through these woods and I froze.

"Yes...Yes please hide my dearest love and best of friends. All it takes is one bite from any one of us on this night and you will have the same immortality; but feel the same Fate of the curse of the silver moon." Dorian said breathless as he dropped down and then rose to his hands and knees while he screamed.

I had to back away as I heard and watched his rib bones break and stretch abnormally; causing his body to shake violently. His spine cracked gruesomely now. In the same bloody fashion as his ears; his body's pale blue flesh was extending and started peeling.

I was terrified but couldn't stop watching as he turned again to me while his raw muscles ripped from the new black furry coat erupting. In silent horror, I watched my love's beautiful purple eyes enlarge and pop full of juices. His eyes had turned into enormous glowing wolf eyes the color of his heart centered rubies. His long blond hair had fallen out but the golden crown still sat on his head even through all these changes.

His whole head and legs were changing at the same time and I couldn't stop myself from watching.

His strong legs had enlarged and bent backwards in a sickening cracking sound; as more black fur emerged. A giant black tail emerged from his bottom as he screamed supernaturally from being ripped from his tail bone horrendously. His piercing scream, I was sure, woke the dead and an eerie chill ran down my spine. *Maybe I should be running right now?* My only thought was love and danger but I remained planted in the grass with his glowing eyes fixated on mine.

"I...I can't leave you here to suffer alone. I love you Dorian." I whispered as his giant wolf eyes stayed fixed on me and he stuck his hand out to stop me from coming closer.

Then he screamed much louder as I watched his pale blue flesh now being ripped from his hands and feet. Suddenly his nails were being pushed out of the skin being replaced with enormous sharp claws erupting. I felt faint as I could hear the bones in his hands and feet cracking as they grew larger with the same midnight fur covering them.

Dorian suddenly screamed again as he tilted his head to the moon and I watched his teeth falling to the grass. Meanwhile, I couldn't stop watching in horror the magic of the darkness. I could only see partially his face tearing and his skull enlarging with the sickening cracking of his bones. His giant wolf snout erupted along with destroying his perfect dimpled chin and his loud scream changed to a horrific howl that echoed throughout the field.

My breath had escaped me as he made a long supernatural howl again right before lowering his head and slowly turning to me. His eerie predator eyes were on me fully as he growled and stood up.

I felt my heart beat speed up and my breath get caught somewhere in the pit of my churning stomach. There was nothing between us as I stood only a small distance away from him. I could even feel his hot breath that smelt of berries and lovely mead; and not like the death I imagined a monster's breath to smell like.

When he took a step towards me, I continued to be frozen as our eyes remained in each other's. I didn't know how much of Dorian was still in there and how much was the darkness. But I didn't care. I had always believed that love conquers all and I believed in our love. So even with my heart racing I stood there before him as he moved slowly closer in the blood moon's light.

꧁꧁꧁꧁

CHAPTER 22

ALORA

Suddenly, we both heard tree branches breaking from behind me and I turned from Dorian to look. The tall figure's golden crown sat on his proud temple in the glow of the red moonlight. I gasped as I saw the figure clad in golden armor with the familiar royal red crest on his chest plate and his arrow aimed in my direction.

"Beast step away from my Daughter so I shall finish you and finally be rid of the darkness that haunts these woods." His authoritative voice boomed across the field.

"You have no right to rid anything from these woods. You have crossed the border of magic and now the darkness will welcome you in its sweet finale embrace." Dorian spoke and gave me chills as his voice was supernaturally deeper and laced with malice.

"Daddy what are you doing here?" I said now upset at this confrontation between Dorian and my Father.

"I am all that is left of the massacre of soldiers and werewolves tonight; not more than a field past these woods. I heard the call and hunted you here to this very spot. I am taking my Daughter back Prince Dorian and shall not be stopped no matter how many more of your kind I kill. I couldn't kill you the last time I tortured you with the whip but I have grew wiser since the last time I captured you. I have silver tipped arrows and even though I know one will not kill you; many in your heart will. Then there is my silver broad sword to finish the job and do you through after I cut your magical head off." My Father said more vicious than I have ever heard him speak and I was still in shock as his bloodied armored glove extended to reach for me.

I was frozen to the spot out of love and trying to figure out what was about to happen; and in trying to quickly come up with a solution. My heart knew a harsh truth though. This was going to end in tragedy and I couldn't stop this but I had to try.

"Please Father I implore you to put down your weapon. I am in love with Prince Dorian. He is the true ruler of these woods and my heart. I could not live in a world where he ceased to exist. I would rather be punished a thousand deaths over and over; even to have his hand in mine and his lips to mine in an eternal kiss for all the days of my life." I said as I tasted my uncontrollable salty tears.

"You my child are talking like you are under witchcraft and look at you. You are dressed as a peasant, in a poor man's long shirt undergarments, under the blood of the full moon. Can't you see Prince Dorian's poisonous sorcery has tainted your feelings? I should have punished him further when I had a chance. I should have known his love-sick magic couldn't be stopped." My Father raged.

"You knew of his love for me? What treachery has fallen upon your heart my Father? You would rather lie than admit Prince Dorian had saved my life with love magic. Do you even know that if it weren't for

Dorian I would be an outcast right now? Tell me Father would you have slain me? Would you have abandoned me these past six years just to finally seek revenge now? If you slay Dorian then you will have to slay me thrice Father. You shall have to slay me once as your only Daughter; twice as your Princess and heir; and thrice in killing the only happiness and joy out of my very existence. Would your revenge satisfy an empty kingdom?" I said and heard the tremor in my voice.

"I cannot believe you hated him just because he is magical and in love with me. Was it just too absurd for a dark woodland elf Prince to actually be good and kind?" I said full of tears and thought about how overprotective and sometimes brain-dead my loving Father was.

"He cannot possible love you Alora. He is a beast of unfeeling born from the womb of darkness. He is a cruel stain upon the sunshine of the world. Please stop blocking the arrow Alora. You must step aside now." My Father said and his voice was loud but much calmer than before.

"Your Majesty my heart has loved Alora since the very first moment I met her in these same woods. We do not have to fight. I want what is best for her; even at my hearts demise. We were on route to your castle. I was bringing her home to you and your kingdom. I do not wish her to be an outcast in this cruel world too." Dorian spoke much deeper than I had ever heard before as I turned to see the giant werewolf of his massive stature; that now gently stepped in front of me.

"No, Dorian I love you. Please Father I beg you not to kill my heart which beats outside of my chest and stands before you in darkness. Please Daddy do not kill my best friend and the love of my life." I said as I moved back in front of Dorian extending my arms wide with my back against his long muscular torso covered in soft fur.

"Alora I have humored your indulgence and need for dragon and elf toys from the market. I even banned them from the castle but knew you held on to the elf wind chimes by your window. I knew of all the hidden fairytales and dark fantasy novels scattered about your room. But this is reality and there are dark creatures in this world. You do not need to tempt the darkness any more than you have. If you do not go with me tonight you will have a hard life. Even your royal blood could not stop the ridicule of hard seasons that your future will hold." My Father said and I was shocked as my Father's eyes glistened; even with his arrow and chin aimed high.

"I knew it from the moment he breathed life into the stillness of your body. I had stumbled upon you both and watched how desperately he tried to save you; even giving a piece of his own heart ruby so that you would live. I saw the love he gave you that day and it frightened me. Here was a dark creature that I was taught to hate. Stories of malice that were told by my Father and his Father; and had been passed down. I was taught that dark woodland elves sucked the very life out of humans. But with my own eyes I had seen the opposite. Prince Dorian had saved you out of the purest love magic. And I couldn't let my heart be right; not when my Father and my mind have always known what was best for the kingdom. I saw the way you looked at him and the way he looked at you. So I had to eradicate him and then outlaw magic from our kingdom. I created the Peace Treaty only because I knew I was willing to sacrifice your true love and marry you to another. Then I broke the accords as Dorian kept trying to contact you. He was still a boy and I had almost killed him." My Father spoke and then lowered his arrow.

"Oh Daddy, how could you?" I gasped.

"I did what I thought was best. I was already losing your mother to the plague. You were only thirteen. I could not lose you to true love's kiss. I was not ready for that as a Father or a King. Your future was to unite kingdoms of human harmony and glory. And in that instant all my plans were derailed. Since then it has been suitors and suitors of Prince's; and no one has ever compared. I know this. I just wasn't ready to let my heart know it had been right all along." My Father said and I embraced him.

As he kissed my forehead he whispered; "I love you my little Princess and darling Daughter. All I have ever wanted was for your happiness my child. You grew up so fast; I am sorry for not trusting what my heart and eyes had always told me about Prince Dorian. And I am sorry Dorian for torturing you and hunting you all these past six years." My Father said as he embraced me.

I whispered; "I love you Daddy."

Then we heard the wolf howls coming from across the woods and I turned to Dorian as his glowing red eyes looked soft. He was so patient in regards to my Father that it stirred my soul in melting over him even more.

"Your Majesty the past is the past. I could never hate you because the same loving blood that runs through Alora's veins runs through yours. But the blood moon is high and the others are coming. They will not let you live after the attack that has just befallen our pack brothers. I am the Alpha and King of the werewolves, but blood and vengeance is necessary unless..." Dorian spoke and we hung off his words as the howling was getting louder.

"Unless what Prince Dorian?" My Father asked as I stood there baffled at what could be imposed.

"I will let you live if you let me have you Daughters hand in marriage. I wish your blessing." Dorian said so deep I almost fainted out of pure rapture from his request.

"But you will be penniless. You will be nothing more than forest peasants of the cold woods. No one will show you kindness. Why would you want that for her?" He asked perplexed now.

"I promise you she will never be penniless. I will take care of her with every fiber of my being. No one will ever harm her in my care. I will love her forever, your Majesty. She holds the wealth of my heart and I will always do anything to provide for her needs. Please let her have that forever love that the mortal world can never give her." Dorian's supernatural voice was so desirable I was swooning but I could tell my Father was thinking.

"Let your Daughter be happy and marry for true love. Give me your blessing for your Daughter's hand in marriage. No Prince will love her as much as I have and always will." Dorian deeply said and I couldn't stop my tears flowing.

I looked to my Father standing there looking down as Dorian and I waited. When he raised his head I saw his proud tears as he extended his hand to Dorian. Dorian shook his hand vigorously and his hand glowed with a red mist. My Kingly Father was all smiles, as we all were, but he stopped for one moment of reflection.

"You have my blessing but I worry about both of your futures. I will do everything in my power to change the laws for you and the other kingdoms of magic." My Father said and I had never seen him so admirable and more magnanimous in the light of the blood moon.

I rushed to him and hugged him tight. He seemed more humble than I had ever seen him as he embraced me back. His Majesty, my Father, was the strongest man I had ever known until the day I met Prince Dorian.

Dorian's strength was easy to see. It came from the immense love he held in compassion for every living thing. I was more jubilant than words could express as I felt Dorian give my Father and I a massive hug; holding us both in his huge arms.

"Prince Dorian you aren't going to lick my face now are you? I did have the servants polish my armor before battle and would hate to get the war blood mixed with drool." My Father asked and I just rolled my eyes as Dorian supernaturally chuckled.

"No your Majesty, however I reserve the right to bequeath my bride's face with drool and kisses in the moonlight." Dorian deeply said and immediately I felt his huge, rough wolf tongue against the whole side of my face and laughed.

"Husband or not, I do not want my hair to be soaked my werewolf dearest." I said as I moved his mouth gently away to stop his assault of loving kisses.

I was blushing as I looked over to my Father who looked in good spirits as he chuckled. Then I thought about Dorian's real kiss and how I could kiss his lips whenever I wanted, for the absolute rest of our lives. I sighed heavenly.

🌾🌾🌾🌾

CHAPTER 23

DORIAN

I could hear the other wolves howling in vengeance and I gave a louder, deeper howl that silenced them. Being the King and Alpha sure had its perks. I would check in on them later when we hunted. Then I gave another long sweet howl about my engagement; and the blessing that would stop the war between us and the humans. There were happy short wolf calls next and it made me smile; however my new Father-in-Law looked a little frightened as the howling shook him.

"Your Majesty we should go. I just called off the others and told them of your blessing and my engagement. They are happy for this cheerful news. Oh and none of the werewolves died, in fact we gained your army as new brethren." I could not help but smile even with my eerie voice I was lighthearted and deeply chuckled; but the King frowned.

I let out another long primal howl and heard the others still hidden in the forest, call out.

"But my blade was silver and all of our arrows. How can this be?" My Father-in-Law asked as we walked the path to his kingdom.

"Well they had told me something about checking your blacksmith that had pocketed the silver and used a polished metal instead." I said deeper and shook my head at the deception.

"That blackheart how dare he be so dubious. But Dorian, what did you say to them in that last howl?" My new Father-in-Law asked as we continued to walk.

"I told them you were not to be harmed because you are family." I said and I swore I had never seen a King choke back so many tears.

"I shall say goodnight to you Daddy. Please come and visit us. The countryside is very peaceful. It will be good for your health." Alora said as I watched them hug in farewell.

"But Daughter it is nightfall and the full moon is high. How will you ever find your way?" My new Father-in-Law asked and I looked at Alora lovingly and smiled as I heard her whistle.

The giant wolf came barreling out of the bushes running straight to her with kisses and his giant tail wagging as my new Father-in-Law froze.

"Father meet Indigo. He is always protecting us and he is just a big puppy full of love. I know he will take me back to the oak tree home and then I can wait there until my darling husband comes home." Alora said and hugged me so tight I felt my heart flutter.

She whispered to me; "My love come home quickly. I shall be waiting in the dry ferns."

As soon as the words left her sweet lips I almost fainted in pure rapture. Here I was this big scary monster and the graceful woman of my dreams had me wrapped around her finger. If she wanted me to pick her thousands of roses in the moonlight I would drop everything at her request; all for her radiant smile. She was simply the air I breathed and the stardust of magic my soul needed forever.

🌿🌿🌿🌿

CHAPTER 24

ALORA

As I stood there waving at the two greatest men in my life, I felt incredibly euphoric. Then I felt my skin starting to burn like I had rubbed my whole arm in stinging nettles. My arm actually felt on fire as I looked down and gasped at the blood across my flesh.

There was a deep bloody scratch running down the length. Then I gasped again as I seen the dozens of magical rose bushes with spikey thorns jutting out. *I wonder how I had not been pricked before? I must really be in the Goddess Fortuna's good graces for only this small wound that could have been worse.* I thought as I continued to smile while walking with Indigo in the blood moon's light.

❁❁❁❁

CHAPTER 25

DORIAN

My heart hurt as I heard the new werewolf's cries and it immediately made the black fur on my neck stand up. It chilled me to the bone. I quickly said farewell to my new Father-in-Law as he took a secret-not-so-secret passage to get inside the castle. Before he left he shook my hand again. His tears made my eyes well up as he patted my back and said; "My Boy I promise to change the laws and will be there for you from this day forward."

"Thank you your Majesty you are very gracious; and thank you for your blessing." I said as he gave me a quick hug.

"You can call me Dad or Father now. We are family. I expect a royal wedding to help plan, but I am honoring your wedding under the moon tonight. I shall see you both soon. Farewell my Son." He said just before he slipped into the passage into the castle and I was happy until I heard the wolf cry.

Then I dropped to all fours and ran to the lake in the soul of the forest where the new werewolf howled again. I could hear the fear in her half-hearted howl that ended in a whimper. I howled long and true of the love in my heart I had for her. *Damn it, I shouldn't have kissed Alora's face over and over. When she lifted my mouth away from her, for one moment I thought my teeth had nicked her and I thought for a second I tasted blood. But she never said anything so I thought I had just imagined it all. I mean accidents happen all the time, but I should have been more careful. Tonight is a full blood moon. It only happens every so many years. I should have been more careful.* I thought as I ran through the forest to find her.

I howled to soothe her. Then I heard a deep growl as I came out of the bushes and into the clearing.

"It was an accident my love. My fangs must have scrapped your arms either when I was licking you, or one of the times we were embracing. It was never meant to happen." I said and got off all fours and walked to her.

Her wolf eyes were glowing and a stunning blue. She was even more beautiful as a werewolf. As an Alpha I tried to calm my thoughts about any other werewolf even thinking about my soon-to-be wife. *I don't want to bite someone's head off, but I might.* I thought as I tried to stop lusting after Alora but she was even more captivating.

"Dorian I am a werewolf now. What will my Father think? He just gave us his blessing." She said as I held her and smelt her lovely black fur that held a scent of roses and lavender.

"Well my dear maybe…Maybe we could just bite him? I mean, I am just putting it out there. I am sure he would love to run wild through the forest. Plus, there are all the health perks; and the never dying bit I am sure he would love." I said in my eerie voice that I was trying to make sound more lighthearted but it just could not happen when I was in my werewolf form.

"You mean you want him to suffer my dearest." She said in almost a growl as I stole a quick wolf kiss.

"Yes it hurts, but it only hurts for a mere moment; and especially if someone is watching. But the magic is forever as is our pack. I will introduce you to them all after we hunt; and be wed by the fairy priest tonight my Queen." I said as I held her tight and she held me; keeping her head close to my chest.

"But Dorian I am frightened." She whispered and it took my breath away.

"But why Alora? You are still you on the inside. I can still see your kind heart." I said as I held her tighter.

"But look at me. I am a monster. I am hideous." She whispered with tears and then I felt my heart break.

"Actually, you are the most gorgeous creature I have ever met. It was easy to be struck by cupid's arrow in your presence. When I was thirteen I knew this and I know this as I stand in awe of your perfect presence in the blood of the full moon's light. You never needed my ruby to make yourself more enigmatic and more spellbinding. You have always been." I said and she looked at me like I had the galaxies in my eyes; and I did, but only for her.

I knew this as we stood there together in a warm embrace with our large tails wrapping each other. I was just magnetically pulled to her always. I tried to deny it for so long. But as I stood there; I just knew she was the one that completed me. I never needed my ruby back – my heart had been hers alone since the very first moment I seen her angelic face in the sunshine of the meadow.

🌾🌾🌾

CHAPTER 26

ALORA

Peacefully, I awoke with the dawn of the sun creeping over the trees. Dorian had been holding me tight and it took me a moment to realize his naked body was covering mine. He snored so heavenly I couldn't help but grin as we lay there while the birds sang.

I looked around and felt happy; even with all the tufts of white and gray fur. There was all this rich blood in little splatters surrounding us. I felt freedom for the first time in my life. My heart was bursting at the seams as I looked at the golden ring back on my finger and remembered our wedding night.

His gentle pale blue hand on my waist made me smile wider. He wore his matching ring again and it melted my heart. Suddenly I heard his sweet murmurs of waking as he breathed in my hair.

"Oh Dorian, I love you so much." I whispered as I started kissing him.

"I love you too Alora. You really are the air I breathe and my sacred light in the darkness." He said now breathless from all my oxygen stealing kisses.

"I never knew what I wanted before Dorian. But this is it. I never wanted you to be alone. But now we are together and you don't ever have to be alone. This is everything I have dreamt of; well minus the dead rabbits but they were surprisingly good raw." I said and giggled as he kissed me.

"You are everything I have wished for and prayed to the Universe to bring me in a soulmate. I love you Alora, my absolutely alluring wife." Dorian whispered and he seemed to glow as he kissed me.

"I love you Dorian with all of my heart." I whispered as we lay there kissing and then Dorian lifted his head looking around.

"My Love we should probably get going and get cleaned up before any villagers with pitch forks come." He said and then chuckled as he helped me up.

"Pitchforks my dear?" I was completely baffled.

"Well my darling, we will have to pay back those sheep we ate last night." He said and smiled as I took his hand and we walked side by side.

"Oh Dorian, I thought that was part of my lovely dream I had." I said and blushed as I was walking with my dashing husband nude into the bushes.

We were filthy from the forest floor, the meadow, and all the blood. But I could not be any happier as I thought about all the lovely babies we were going to have.

"I was so happy last night I indulged us in an after midnight feast. The rabbits were the dessert." He said and chuckled again and it felt good to hear his handsome laughter.

This morning something was different about me; and I could not describe all the loving emotions I had as I looked at Dorian in the sunlight. It felt like some beautiful waking dream. I felt more than euphoric to hold his hand and be fearless as we walked to the enchanted lake.

I felt a prevailing change in my soul and it wasn't because I had conquered my fear of the water. It was because with Dorian I felt so unconditionally loved. His hand in mine meant I could do anything. I could not have known how amazing his friendship and strength would be to me. His powerful love surrounded me and made me feel always safe and cared for.

We could finally be free together and have our true love's happiness forever.

♥The End♥

EPILOGUE

ALORA

"Was it was really necessary to summon me with your guards Father? Alora and I would have come freely with the children to see you at your request. I have felt your presence on me for these last few years. But you have never needed the shadows. You have always been welcomed at my table and in our home. My door has always been open to your closed royal heart, my King." Dorian spoke as the guards held him using their spears at his throat before the King ordered them to leave without speaking; just a nod.

"It was one thing to witness your transformation in the full moons light but to marry a human has always been forbidden Dorian. Might I remind you; you are the Prince and my heir to the throne. But no formalities will matter now. I summoned you here because I am perishing my Son and I did not know how to request your presence any other way. I have lived hundreds of years on this grand earth that you shall inherit and treasure; with your wife and my grandchildren." I watched as the ancient elf King coughed and Dorian helped him sit up with pillows.

Then Dorian gave him a glass filled with some purple potion. The King's prehistoric eyes immediately went to me as I stood off in the shadows with our children. The children were silent in a knowing of the great King's presence and illness.

The castle was such a grand temple with golden pillars and high ceilings. Even the gray floor stones seemed extravagant as they had elvish scribing and symbols on each stone. I was in awe of the exquisiteness as I watched nature blossoming in the structure. There were magnificent trees growing inside the castle and different colored wild rose bushes growing everywhere. There were fairies sprinkling spread pixie dust on flowers to help open blooms. It was the most spectacular kingdom and castle I had ever seen.

"Please let me pass my magic and wisdom to you my Son. Please forgive me for wasting the precious time I could have been a part of your found happiness and loving family. I was raised in a primordial world of tradition and it was unheard of for a dark woodland elf to be cursed. Though as we speak; there are over half of our subjects that have wandered to that very lake and transformed. There is this unusual change in my subject's souls that radiates a freedom of nature. I could never have believed the connection until I witnessed your children playing in the meadow." The grand elf King said and coughed again as Dorian passed the glass to him and he took a quick sip.

I watched with silent tears as Dorian's hand was in his Fathers. I brought our three children closer to the fierce warrior elf King's bed where he was propped up with golden pillows. Even in his death the King looked majestic and honorable.

"Your Majesty this is Prince Henry; he is four. And this is Princess

Annabelle; she is three. The little one there is Prince Alfred and he is two and quite mischievous." I said in complete happiness and Dorian rubbed my obvious baby bump then gave me a sweet kiss.

The ancient King gasped as he looked at the pale blue children and saw their small golden crowns on their heads that matched his giant crown. They all had purple eyes; pale blue skin; pointy ears and fanged smiles. With their blonde hair they matched the King completely. As if on cue, to some invisible question that hung in the air; the three children sat down and showed their forearms to the King. The ancient King placed his forearm to theirs and Dorians. All of them had the royal birthmark which was the form of the constellation Pisces. It was only bestowed upon the true royals and heirs to the throne.

The King gasped again as he picked up Prince Alfred and the small child placed his tiny hands on the massive golden branches of the crown on the Kings head. The old elf King's massive crown of gold was encrusted with emeralds, diamonds, and rubies.

I looked at my beautiful children that looked just like their Daddy and their Grandfather; and I smiled.

"They are dark woodland elves entirely. How can this be? Alora are you not human?" The King said as Prince Alfred hugged him and he hugged him back.

"Your Majesty it would appear a very long time ago our kingdoms interacted enough that I held elf blood in my veins." I said as I smiled warmly to Dorian's Father.

The ancient King sat there amazed as Princess Annabelle held his hand.

"Dorian I foresee the future of the Graystar kingdom merged with the kingdom of Camelot-Gardenia. I see the harmonious relationship you have brought both kingdoms and the centuries of peace to come. I just wish in my arrogance I had not waited so long to meet your beautiful human wife and your lovely woodland elf children.

"Father they are neither woodland elf nor human. We are family. Alora and I shall bring another child into this wonderful world in less than three months and that child shall be loved just as much." Dorian said and kissed me.

Then he gently patted my baby bump and kissed my stomach. I took the ancient Kings hand and placed it gently on my baby bump and his purple eyes glowed as he felt the baby move to where his hand was. We both didn't say any words as he kindly smiled to me and I smiled back in pure content.

"You will be a just ruler Prince Dorian, my dear Son. Your kindness is what my reign lacked. I just wished I could have seen this bright vision of the future in person." The ancient King said as a golden tear rolled down his cheek.

"Father it does not have to be this way. You could live forever with us in this new utopia. Your illness would be taken away." Dorian said as he grabbed his Father's hand and it brought a few tears to my eyes.

"How my Son? I can feel the change from my soul turning gray. I thought the plague in the human's world would not reach our beloved kingdom. But it did unfortunately and painfully. I lost my best friend and your mother two years ago now. I have suffered alone and now the illness has come to take me beyond." The King said and coughed as Dorian gave him some more of the strange purple liquid.

"Tonight I can cure you. This year is a very rare and special year astrologically. Under normal circumstances; blood full moons happen every three years. But there are four this year. Tonight there will be a blood full moon. If you let me cure you then our kingdom can flourish without the poison running through your veins. Please Father let me gift you this darkness out of love. No matter the past between us; I have always felt your loving presence through the years. Let me save you with my love for you and our kingdom." Dorian spoke as his golden tears rolled down his cheeks.

The ancient King's eyes welled up as he looked at Dorian and I watched both their heart rubies glowing. Instinctively I knew what was about to happen as I gently rubbed my baby bump and a few tears escaped my happy eyes.

"Come children you can see your Grandfather in a couple of hours when we all will play in the full moon's light." I gently said and kissed my Father-in-Law on the cheek as he weakly smiled to me.

Then I took the children outside the King's private quarters; after they had all kissed their Grandfather in farewell. I hoped that Dorian could persuade his Father to rule a little longer so we could enjoy the countryside before our royal duties would begin again.

We had already changed my Father a few months ago and he had quite enjoyed paying off villagers for the sheep every month.

Some royal families had traditions but I feel ours was the best. Who could have known running in the shadows of the moon could bring so much light and unity. Our future was full of freedom and true everlasting love.

My life really was a perfect happily ever after fairytale.

Thank goodness for Dorian's lovely blood moon kisses.

🌾🌾🌾

ACKNOWLEDGMENTS

I would really like to express my sincere gratitude to; The Universe, my fans, family, and friends. Its fine people like you that give struggling authors a chance. Thank you again!

I would also like to thank my mechanics and my friends Eric Heldman and Jay Flowers at Cormier's Good Year Obsentia, in Quinte West, Ontario. Thank you for always being great friends and taking care of my car. I am so appreciative that you are lights in the world and practice random acts of kindness every day. Thank you again for not suing me for killing off your characters in future novels! Their website is here if you want some kind individuals helping you with your auto needs and are in the Quinte West Area: https://www.trentontire.ca/

Thank you for reading!   I really hope you have liked my story. Please add a short review and let me know what you thought!

And always let your light shine bright!

ABOUT THE AUTHOR

A.L. Secord is a pen name for the author APRIL SECORD. She enjoys many genres. But she is most passionate about Dark Fantasy Romance. She loves learning new things, and occasionally burning food for the ones she loves. She is an author, a proud mother, and an avid adventurer of the unknown; on her many pursuits for greater happiness and Bigfoot.

A DARK FANTASY ROMANCE

THE HOUSE
WINS

APOCALYPTIC FRIENDS TO LOVERS

A.L. SECORD

A CHRISTMAS DARK FANTASY ROMANCE

FOREST LOVE

BROKEN VAMPIRE PRINCE

A.L. SECORD

THE LAST KING

EVIL TASTES GOOD

A.L. SECORD

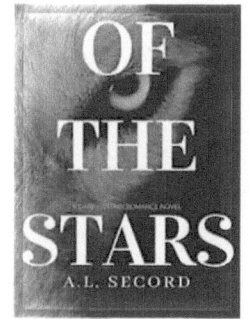

Books by A.L. SECORD: